GRAHAM PARK

A TWISTED TIMBERS THRILLER

A NOVEL BY

Kevin M. Moehring

This one is for my daughter Mira, who says my books are boring because there are no fairies, princesses or unicorns. Love you bug!

ISBN: 978-0-692-98167-2

Chapter 1

If you are not from the Northwest, then you have probably never heard of the town of Twisted Timbers. If you have never heard of the town, then you have no idea of the reputation it has of being one of the most peaceful small towns in America. Ever since the fire that destroyed the sawmill, the town has become one of the most popular vacation destinations for people looking to connect with nature. The remoteness of the town has made it the perfect getaway for families looking for peace and quiet.

For kids who grow up in the small Oregon town, the lack of excitement in the town has led their imaginations to create myths and urban legends. Every child has heard the stories of how the old mill burned down and how the ghosts of the workers who were killed still haunt the area. The most popular legend is the one that focuses around Graham Park, the amusement park located about ten miles east of town.

As the story goes, one of the men who died in the mill fire visits the park on a regular basis. He waits there in the hopes that he will get to spend another day riding the rides with his young son, who at the time of his death was just an infant. Details of the haunting of Graham Park vary depending on who is telling the story but usually involve the Ferris Wheel spinning around, with its bright lights shining, long after the park is closed for the season. Several people have filed reports in the past claiming to see the bright lights shining while they traveled down the main highway.

There has never been any hard evidence that Graham Park or the town of Twisted Timbers is haunted but that has never stopped the topic from being repeatedly discussed during recess at school or from being told around the campfire during boy scout trips. Most of the kids in the area have been to Graham Park during the summer months and have never seen anything they would consider odd or could be labeled as haunted. Many of their fondest memories include the first time they rode the roller coaster or getting their first kiss atop the very Ferris Wheel that is the subject of many of these myths. Twisted Timbers is the kind of place were families live for generations, with the children often living very similar lives as their parents did years before.

As the winter is slowly melting away in the area and the trees are beginning to bloom, most residents are taking up the tasks of getting the town ready for the upcoming tourist season. Since the saw mill closed, tourism has been the leading source of revenue for the town. The natural beauty of the area has drawn hikers and campers to the area for generations. Nestled deep in the Oregon forests along the Nehalem River, Twisted Timbers is sixty miles away from the nearest interstate. The remoteness of the town adds to the feeling of seclusion which many people are looking for when they visit the area. Graham Park is the lone tourist attraction in the area that does not allow its visitors to feel closer to nature. A family trip to the theme park is usually the highlight of their stay in the small, secluded town.

It is unlikely that the people that visit the town, as an escape from their hectic lives, have any knowledge of the sorted past of Twisted Timbers. They would never allow their kids to ride the Ferris Wheel at Graham Park if they knew what the town residents often said about the large metal structure. They would not be so quick to camp in the woods that surround the town if they knew the odd sounds that often break through the silence on chilly winter nights. They would never come to Twisted Timbers if they had ever heard the stories that the town youth would make up to scare one another.

Chapter 2

Mitch Thompson grew up in Twisted Timbers and unlike most of his peers, he stayed in the town even after he graduated high school. In the three years since he graduated, he has worked with his father, the town sheriff, and has hated every second of it. He quickly learned to detest the tourist season and the increased responsibility that came along with it. On a typical day, Mitch would be relegated to traffic control outside of Graham Park or along Main Street. Nothing exciting ever happened and for a twenty-one-year-old, excitement was all that he craved.

Sheriff Bill Thompson was getting older by the day and Mitch knows that one day he would be counted on to take over the duties as sheriff. This was not something he looked forward to. This past winter was hard on his father. The old man has arthritis in both of his knees, making it hard for him to walk. Some days,

Bill would never even get out of bed. This allowed Mitch several opportunities to practice the duties that his father would normally take care of on a daily basis. The paperwork was by far the least popular task that Mitch was forced to deal with, sometimes spending long hours sitting at his desk.

Now that spring is quickly approaching, Mitch has taken it upon himself to step into the role of preparing the town for the tourists. This includes making sure the highway that leads into town is free of debris and all of the temporary street signs that direct tourists to the local attractions have all been mounted. If there is one thing that his three years of experience has taught him, it's that tourists will always get lost, even when there are giant signs pointing them to their destination.

As he makes his way north on Highway 25, the road that leads visitors to Graham Park, the sun is slowly starting to set behind the trees. Views like these are what brings the people to the area. The orange and red sky cast the entire road in front of him in a warm glow. As he nears the location for the turn for Graham Park, Mitch slowly pulls his truck to the shoulder and turns on his hazard lights. As he climbs out of the cab, he reaches into the bed of the truck and pulls out the last of his signs. A few turns of his wrench and the new sign is added to the existing street sign and Mitch returns to his truck.

As he does every time he is in this area, he decides to make a pass around the park to make sure everything is as it should be. He has heard all of the rumors and urban legends before, but he was never a believer. Growing up as the son of the town sheriff has made him more of a realist and not one that puts too much stock into the rambling of little boys on the playground. The sun has completely set now and only his headlights lead the way on the pavement leading to Graham Park. The large pine trees along the side of the road have always hidden the entrance to the park. In fact, during the day when the lights of the park cannot be seen, many tourists miss the driveway and are several miles down the road before they realize they have made an error.

Mitch has made this drive several times, although he is having a tough time remembering the last time. He can't remember if he has made a single trip out to the park since he took down the signs at the end of last season. Maybe he was too caught up in dealing with his ailing father or maybe it just slipped his mind. There is no other reason for him to be heading in this direction and with the park closed for the season, there was never a call to the sheriff's office in the winter months. As he rounds the final bend before the gravel driveway to the park he is greeted by an unusual sight. He slams on the brakes to the truck and stops right in the middle of the road. He has not seen another motorist in the last twenty minutes on this baron stretch of road.

Mitch gets out of the truck and stands beside his open door, staring into the distance. If he wasn't here seeing it with his own eyes, he would not believe it to be true. Breaking through the darkness, like a neon light in a dark alley, the Ferris Wheel shines brightly. The lights flicker in the distance. The reds, greens, yellows and blues are all at full power and Mitch is left speechless and trembling. Even now that he is standing here staring at it, he doesn't believe it. He watches for a full minute or two as the cars on the ride make their usual loop around. His heart instantly beats faster, fearing that the rumors he has heard for years is true.

Chapter 3

Standing alone in the middle of the road, with his truck running, Mitch is left wondering what he should do next. He reaches into his pocket and pulls out his pack of cigarettes. His father has begged him to quit for years now but Mitch has refused. The fact is that he has control over his habit and only lights one up after a long day and before bed. This, however, is surely reason enough to take a few drags. The feeling of the nicotine hitting his body and the warm smoke filling his lungs is enough to calm him down and allow his heart to return to a normal pace.

Like everyone else who grew up in Twisted Timbers, he has heard the stories of the Ferris Wheel operating on its own. Never has there been any proof of this actually happening, until now. The young man stands in awe at the sight of the lights rotating in the complete darkness. No other rides in the park seem to be turned on. There is not a single car to be found in the large gravel parking lot. Are the stories he has heard all throughout his childhood actually true?

He hates that he has no idea what to do about the situation and reluctantly pulls out his cell phone. He doesn't want to call his father, but this is most definitely a unique situation and he could use some advice. Service in this area is normally shady at best but even with the storm that is due around midnight, Mitch is relieved that his call goes through without issue. It takes several rings for his father to answer on the other end. Sheriff Thompson has the voice of a movie star hero, the deepness of it has always made his words seem to come across with much more meaning.

"Dad, I need you to listen to me. I know it's late and I'm sorry for calling but I need some advice. I was hanging the last of the tourist signs and decided to turn down Graham Road and take a look at the park. When I got closer, I could see the lights from the Ferris Wheel were on. What do I do?" Mitch hears himself say the words and instantly feels like an idiot. He tells himself that if he heard one of the other deputies tell him the same story, he would probably laugh and hang up the phone.

"Not again, Mitch you're going to have to check it out. Call for backup and don't go into the park until they arrive. You got it? Do not go in until you have backup." His father did not find it funny at all, in fact his tone was more serious than Mitch would have expected. His father hung up the phone as soon as he finished talking and allowed no time for another question from Mitch.

Did he just say, 'not again'? What is that supposed to mean? Maybe the stories the kids told on the playground were true. He is certain that if there was ever anything big that happened at the park, he would have heard about it at one time or another during his childhood. Mitch is speaking out loud as if there were several people standing around in a group. He looks down at his cell phone and presses the button to completely end the call with his father.

Like his father had instructed, Mitch dials the cell phone again and calls the station. He knows that both Donovan and Johnson are on-duty and they would race out to the park as soon as they could. Neither of the two

11

deputies believed what he told them, but they did as they were told. They were not going to ignore an order from the son of the town sheriff, even if they have several years more experience. The station was at least a half an hour drive away and Mitch was going to be alone until then.

He climbs back into his truck and puts it into gear, makes the wide turn onto the driveway and drives through the gravel parking lot of Graham Park. He allows the truck to idle him closer to the front gate until he gets to the end of the gravel and the beginning of the cement walkway that leads visitors through the gates. He decides it may be a good idea to spin the truck around and back in close to the gate, in case there is a need for a quick escape.

Once he is happy with the positioning of the truck, he slowly exits the vehicle. Mitch opens the tailgate and takes a seat on it. Lighting up another cigarette happens without much thought as he stares at the lights of the Ferris Wheel again. The ride has always been one of the main attractions at the park and is the first thing visitors see as they enter the parking lot. Now, with its lights shining, it rises far above the wrought iron gate. The large metallic letters that spell out Graham Park look tiny in the shadow of the ride. As he takes the last puff from his cigarette, with no warning at all, the Ferris Wheel stops spinning, and the lights go dark. The only light in the area is now the headlights from his truck, which are now regretfully pointing away from the park. As he climbs down from the bed of the truck, he is certain that he hears something. The sound is coming from far off in the distance, but the silence of the nights in this part of the world make unusual noises almost echo through the darkness.

"What is that? Is there someone on the roller coaster?"

Kevin M. Moehring

Chapter 4

Stuart Johnson and Fred Donovan arrive much quicker than Mitch had expected them to. Not much has happened for the last five minutes and Mitch was never able to hear the sounds that he swore he heard in the moments right after the Ferris Wheel stopped spinning. He was sure he heard the metal chain pulling the passenger car up the giant hill of the roller coaster. From the first time you ever ride a roller coaster, that sound is embedded in your mind as the scariest thing you have ever heard. In the last few minutes the only thing he has been able to hear is the normal sounds of the Oregon wildlife.

His two fellow officers exit the squad car in unison and walk over to where Mitch has parked his truck. There was an extended period of awkwardness as the two deputies look at the now dark ride, then back to Mitch, and again at the ride. He knows what they are thinking and how silly he must look just sitting here staring at a Ferris Wheel that is most definitely not working.

"I know what you're thinking but it was lit up. I am not imagining it. As soon as it shut off, I could have sworn I heard the roller coaster too." Now that he has said it out loud, he realizes how strange it sounds. Everyone knows that the park would not be hosting visitors for another few weeks and the thought that rides would be operating in an obviously vacant amusement park sounds rather silly.

"Have you been drinking on the job again Mitch?" Stuart Johnson has always used his sense of humor as a way to bring a little levity to tense situations. He has been on the force for almost fifteen years now and is considered the next in line to become sheriff, a title that he hopes to avoid at all costs. He enjoys his job but has no plans on increasing his work load.

"I have not been drinking. I know I sound crazy or drunk. The ride was most definitely lit up and operating. We need to go inside and have a look around. I called my father, I mean, I called the sheriff and he told me to get you guys out here before I went in and looked around."

Fred Donovan is now standing on the opposite side of Mitch and is kicking at some of the loose gravel in the parking lot with his cowboy boots. Fred has always considered himself to be a good-looking guy even though he has had zero success with the ladies for as long as Mitch has known him. He is the epitome of bravado on the outside but whenever a skirmish breaks out, he is also the first one to volunteer to be as far away from the action as possible. "Don't you think it might make more sense to come back out here in the morning at first light?"

"Oh man," Mitch jumps down from the tailgate and pulls up on his belt. "Fred, are you a little scared? Afraid there might be some ghosts hanging out in our little town?" Mitch doesn't say another word and returns to the driver's side of his truck. He reaches into the cab and grabs his flashlight and rifle. He sticks the flashlight into the pocket on the back of his jeans, checks the rifle for ammo and slams the door shut. "We sit around here and do nothing all winter and now that there is the first sign of action, you're ready to go off and cry about it?"

"That's not it Mitch but we've all heard the stories about this place and I was hoping to head over to the Bottom Dollar for a few drinks. It's ladies' night and you know how much I love the ladies!" Fred has a grin from ear to ear at the thought of spending the night partaking in his favorite past time, chasing shots and chasing women.

The laughter from Mitch and Stuart comes out as one giant chorus. Fred turns instantly red in the face as his attempts at trying to find a female friend have always been the subject of great ridicule. "It's not about how much you love the ladies, it's about how much the ladies do not love you," Mitch jokes. Grab your flashlights and rifles and let's get going."

Even though Mitch has been to the park dozens of times as a child, the fact that there are no lights on gives the place an ominous feel that makes him uneasy. It may be for personal pride or the fact that he feels the need to constantly impress his father, but Mitch is more than ready to lead the officers into Graham Park. He is not worried about ghosts or spirits but the one line his father uttered on the telephone has him a bit concerned.

If this sort of thing had happened before, and his father was aware of it, what was the end result.

He is certain that if things were too dangerous, his father would not have instructed him to enter the park, even with the other officers. His father has always done things by the book and cautioned on the side of safety, so chances are he would not send his son into a dangerous situation with only two other men to protect him. Stuart and Fred are both great police officers, but they are not the sort of people you would want by your side when you needed to do battle. If it came to writing tickets or directing traffic, then they would be the first names on the list.

The three men, each with a rifle and a flashlight, walk side-by-side toward the main gate of the park. Two giant columns act as bookends and hold the giant letters that spell out the park's name in large letters. The gate is constructed of iron spindles that come to a point at the top of each. A large chain is wrapped loosely around the spot where the two halves of the iron gate meet. Since the owners of the park only live in town during the peak season, they have left the keys to the gate at the police station in case there was ever a need to get in. Mitch fumbles around for the right key and as he reaches to position the lock, he sees it has already been opened. It hangs from two links of chain, one from each end, to make it appear as if everything was secure. In reality, it takes less than three seconds to remove the lock and allow the chain to fall to the ground. Stuart gives the left gate a slight push with his foot and Graham Park, and everything inside, is open to the three men.

Chapter 5

They walk together into the darkness of the park, Mitch in the center, Stuart on the left and Fred on the right. The enormity of the Ferris Wheel looms in front of them and although none of the men want to say anything about it, it welcomes them with an eerie quiet. Each man is shining his flashlight to cover as much ground as they can before moving forward with small hesitant steps. They climb over the turnstiles that would normally count the visitors to the park on a daily basis, and hesitantly cover the fifty or so feet to the front of the large wheel.

"Stuart, you go around the back and check for anything unusual. Fred, you come with me and once we climb the fence, we'll each go around the ride from opposite directions. Make note of anything that looks out of place or doesn't seem to belong. Once you finish the loop, meet back here in front." He uses his flashlight to point out the specifics to the two other deputies as if he has appointed himself in charge of the investigation. The other two men have far more seniority than Mitch, but they have never been eager to take the lead.

"I'm not sure what we are looking for," Fred utters, "this thing looks like it hasn't been run since last fall." The fence surrounding the ride is showing the signs that come with many months of inactivity. The vines have worked their way through the opening in the fence and have laid their claim to the area. The harsh winter months have left much of the black paint on the metal gate needing repair. Even the bright colors of the cars of the Ferris Wheel look worn out and weathered.

"Let's just do our due diligence and if there's nothing to find, we'll be out of here quickly. Then you can get over to the Bottom Dollar for that drink." Once again Mitch has taken control of the situation and tries to act like his father would if he were in the same situation. Even though he doesn't want to be a police officer for the rest of his life, he desperately seeks the approval of his father.

Fred snickers a bit at the last remark, he knows it's just another intentional attack at his lack of success with the ladies. "A drink sounds good," the man replies. "Actually, quite a few drinks sound even better."

Stuart follows the concrete path to the right of the ride and the other two men watch him until the path leads him out of their sight. Mitch nods to Fred and they aim their flashlights toward the gate to the Ferris Wheel. They bypass the long winding rows that would form the line for the riders and opt to take the shortest path and climb the fence near where the ride operator would sit. Mitch clears the fence with a fluid, athletic motion while Fred struggles a bit. He spends several seconds with his legs on either side of the fence, both dangling about six inches from the ground. His crotch is resting on the railing as if he were sliding down the banister of a stairway. After a few seconds of awkward groans and movements, Fred finally decides to go for it and throws his right leg over and slides clumsily off of the railing.

"Boy, I can see the gracefulness that all the ladies rave about. You head that way." Mitch uses his flashlight to point Fred to go counter-clockwise around the ride, while he takes off in the opposite direction. Mitch stops long enough to inspect the control panel the ride operator would use. There is a series of buttons, knobs and switches. He pulls out his notebook, which he was taught early on that every good police officer should carry, and jots down a reminder to ask the park owner if the control panels are usually covered up during the off months.

He continues to follow the vine-covered fence around to the right until he has completed about half of the circle. He is now directly across from where the operator sits and where they just climbed the fence. There is more than enough room to for a person to get close to the inner workings of the ride. He is only a few feet from the levers, gears and chains that make the enormous ride spin so smoothly. The cool night air is filled with the odor of exhaust and oil. A few small steps put him in between two of the brightly colored gondolas, where there are sheets of thin metal that cover the mechanical aspects of the ride. He places his hand on the metal to balance himself, so he can lean in and take a look at the oily parts. It takes a brief second for him to understand what is happening before he removes his hand and lets out an expletive filled rant.

"Mitch, what's going on? I heard you talking like a sailor over here." Fred is now standing directly behind Mitch. "Everything alright?"

"Put your hand on that piece of sheet metal." Mitch is rubbing the inside of his palm and wincing in pain. "Just touch it, don't leave your hand on there too long."

"It's hot. It's really hot. That makes no sense." Fred touches the sheet metal a few times to make sure the sensation he is feeling is legitimate. "What in the world would make that feel so warm?"

Mitch stands up straight and looks around the park once more, then looks right into the eyes of his colleague. "It makes perfect sense if the ride was running tonight. Just like I told you it was. If it was running earlier, and I know it was, that means we are not alone in the park. We need to find out who else is here and why."

Kevin M. Moehring

Chapter 6

The two officers finish inspecting the area directly surrounding the Ferris Wheel and find nothing else abnormal. Mitch is now holding the flashlight in his left hand and has his rifle slung over his shoulder. The time he left his hand on the sheet metal has turned his palm a bright red color and his skin is painful to the touch. Even with the use of only one good hand, Mitch is still able to climb the fence with far more grace than Fred does. Once again, the elder officer has a look on his face like he is stuck on a test question that he doesn't know the answer to. Mitch starts heading away from the ride and a few seconds later he can hear the panting breaths of Fred who is jogging to catch up.

It isn't long before Stuart meets the other two at the front of the ride. "Mitch, I found this behind the ride. It could be something or it could have been left last fall.

There's really no way to tell." Stuart extends his right arm and hands Mitch a ball cap.

He takes the cap and gives it the once over. The bright yellow logo of the University of Oregon is embroidered on the front of the hat, in stark contrast to the forest green coloring of the rest of the material. The back of the hat has been adjusted to fit the head of someone very small, an adult more than likely, but not a very large individual. "Where did you find this? I need to know exactly where it was."

Stuart seems puzzled by the question at first and looks back down the path before responding. "It was on the north side of the ride, about three quarters of the way around the path. Under that side of the wheel, like someone probably lost it while riding the ride."

"Where was it exactly? Was it on the path or did you find it underneath the bushes?" It's times like these that Mitch has been told he can be a bit arrogant and hard to work with. His father has told him numerous times he needs to work on his people skills, but he finds it hard to be patient when Stuart is being oblivious to the importance of the hat.

"It was in the path, right in the middle of the path. If I hadn't seen it and picked it up, chances are I would have stepped on it. I don't see what the big deal is Mitch, it's just a hat. I'm sure kids lose hats on the rides here all summer long." When Mitch gets in one of his moods, the other deputies usually stay their distance. Stuart, in this case, has nowhere else to go and is forced to deal with the full wrath.

"For your information, this hat was not lost last summer. It was probably lost tonight while the ride was running. That's why it's so important for you to remember the details." Mitch pulls out his notebook once more and jots down more details regarding the hat, mainly where it was found and by whom.

Fred chimes in, making an effort to take some of the heat off of his partner, "How do you know it wasn't lost during the summer? I think you may be jumping to conclusions."

"Fred, I know what you're doing. You're a good partner and friend but we need to do everything here by the book. Someone is here, and we need to make sure we cover all our bases. You felt the ride, so you know it had been running at some point tonight."

"Yes, I did. Like you I find that odd but that has nothing to do with the hat that Stuart found." Fred reaches for the ball cap, but Mitch just turns away from him and directs his attention back to Stuart.

"What are you guys talking about? How do you know the ride was operating at some point tonight?" Stuart takes two steps away from the other two and says these words out loud, not directing them at either man in particular. His gaze is affixed over their heads as he studies the Ferris Wheel for any sign of activity.

"The covering to the mechanical part of the ride was very hot, so hot that it burned my palm. For this reason, we can deduct that the ride was operating at some point tonight, and that I'm not crazy for that matter." He stops long enough to let that last point sink in and takes the time to make eye contact with both men before proceeding. "As for this ball cap, I can tell just by looking at it that it was not left here from the summer. Anyone can see that. We had about four feet of snow this year. If this hat would have been left out in the elements for the winter, there would be for more signs of damage. The material is in far too good of shape and the brim looks like it has barely ever been worn, let alone survived an Oregon winter."

"That all makes sense Mitch, but I am not sure. Maybe it was under the branches of one of the tall pine trees over there. The trees are all over the place in this park. Couldn't the hat just have landed in the exact right spot to stay dry?" Stuart sounds more as if he was trying to convince himself, as well as Mitch, that there is nothing out of the ordinary going on at Graham Park, but even a person with as little intuition as he has would know that something just isn't right.

"If it were under the trees it would have been covered in pine straws or sap. There is no evidence of either. This hat was lost recently, maybe even this evening." Mitch finally hands the hat to Fred who again gives it a thorough inspection. "There have been too many signs that there is something going on in here. We need to do a proper investigation. Boys, get ready for a very long night."

Kevin M. Moehring

Chapter 7

Fred Donovan has always been willing to do whatever task is needed as part of the job. Stuart Johnson, on the other hand, would rather sit behind his desk and fill out paperwork until his shift was over. He is in no way cut out for any type of police work other than writing tickets for the cars that are parked illegally on Main Street during the summer months. Now that he is forced to be a part of the threesome that is searching Graham Park, he is less than eager to get started. "You think I should head back to the station and make a few phone calls? I'm sure the feds would be willing to send some people down to help us out."

Mitch looks at him with disgust. The winters in Twisted Timbers are long and cold and lack of anything close to excitement. This is the first real police matter that has arose since September. "That's not going to happen. The park is very big, and we will need all the men we have. Plus, what if this turns out to be nothing? Do you want to be responsible for calling in the boys from Portland over something that we should have handled ourselves?"

"No, not exactly. I'm just not cut out for this kind of stuff. Chasing ghosts and sounds in the night are not the things I signed up for when I took this job." Stuart is already showing the signs of a nervous man who is being forced to do something that is far from his comfort zone.

"You signed up to be a police officer. This is what police officers do. They investigate strange happenings, apprehend the suspects and arrest them." He looks over to Fred in hopes he will give a nod of agreement and take his side. "I don't know what exactly you think you signed up for, but this is what we are supposed to do. We are going to spread out, so we can cover more ground. Every time you enter a new building or ride, or you find something that could be important, I want you to communicate it over the radio. Is that clear?"

Stuart nods in agreement, even though he does it reluctantly. He knows that Mitch is the son of his boss, and he is aware of the fact that how he acts tonight will be relayed to the sheriff whether he likes it or not. Stuart

Johnson has been on the police force for over fifteen years and in all of that time he has never had to carry his rifle. Not even once. The last time it was used was when he went to Portland to take training classes and become re-certified to carry it. Now he grips onto it as if it is the only thing that is keeping him safe from whatever is hiding in the dark.

Mitch is still nursing his sore hand but manages to use the tip of his rifle to point each man in the direction he wants them to head. "Stuart, I want you to head north and check out the kids' area. Fred, you go south and check out the water park and area around it. I'll head straight through, behind the Ferris Wheel and have a look at the midway and the other rides. Stay alert, and remember to use the radio. I don't know who is here, but I have a feeling they are not going to be happy to see us."

Mitch watches as Fred almost skips into action and heads for the water park area. He is heading down the same patch of concrete that he used to circle the Ferris Wheel, except this time when the path forks, he heads left. He disappears behind a row of trees that have been allowed to hang low over the path. A few seconds later, even the glow from his flashlight is no longer visible.

Mitch turns to Stuart and gives him the nodding motion that signals it's time for him to get going too. Although he is reluctant to do so, he finally gets his lanky body moving in the direction of the kids rides. Mitch watches him and can tell he is extremely nervous. His flashlight is darting quickly from side to side. Mitch knows that there is someone uninvited in Graham Park and he prays that it is not Stuart who runs into the person first.

Satisfied that the other two officers are going about their tasks properly, Mitch turns on his flashlight and circles around to the back of the Ferris Wheel. Here the path forms a T with the large, usually well-lit midway. This was always the last stop most visitors would make before exiting the park. The midway is lined with carnival games, arcades and food booths. Mitch stands at the intersection of the two paths and closes his eyes. The time he spent with his grandfather hunting in the woods has taught him the importance of smelling the air for anything that seems out of place.

His mind takes him back to visiting Graham Park as a child. The smells of cotton candy, popcorn and caramel apples always made him smile. He remembers his father always promising that he could have one treat on the way out if he acted properly throughout the day. Mitch would always choose the popcorn, because it was his father's favorite and he knew he could share.

Standing here in the quiet now has brought no unusual smells. The night has turned colder, and the change in temperature has made the tip of his nose red. He opens his eyes and without thinking about it he uses his right hand to rub his nose in an attempt to warm it up. The pain in his hand is excruciating but he refrains from letting out a sound and giving away his position.

He proceeds down the path of the midway in pure silence. Every step that he makes falls softly on the concrete. To the west he can see the lightning off in the distance. The weather guy had said there would be a storm overnight, but Mitch was hoping they could finish this up before it moved in. Using the knowledge that comes from years spent in this part of the country, he knows the storm is still about an hour away.

A few more steps down the midway brings Mitch to the rows of carnival games and video game arcades. Both sides of the walkway are surrounded by the short, wooden buildings. When the park is open, the individual rooms of these buildings are filled with stuffed animals, flashing lights and workers who are trying to convince the visitors that they are guaranteed to win. Now, the openings are covered with sheets of plywood, the lights are all dark and the midway is completely silent.

Mitch shines his flashlight from side to side, he didn't really know if there was a proper technique, but he uses the flashlight as he was trained to do with his pistol. Don't point it anywhere you are not looking was the line the instructor used repeatedly. When he was a kid the thrill of these games sent his heart racing. He remembers how his father told him that most of these games were rigged in favor of the park but that didn't make it any easier for Mitch to bypass them. Near the center of the buildings, and located directly in the middle of the walkway, is a circular hut.

The hut has been boarded up and there are no distinct markings on the outside. Mitch assumes this building operates as a food or beverage vendor when the park is open, but he can't be sure. He decides to walk around the small building and when he reaches the back side, he sees a door. This is when Mitch wishes the owner would leave all the keys to the park, rather than just the one that opens the front gate. The door is closed tightly but he decides to try the handle anyway. A small turn of the knob and he hears the unmistakable sound of the locking mechanism releasing. With the door opened slightly he can see the stream of light that is escaping through the tiny opening. He returns his flashlight to his back pocket and positions his rifle to aim directly at the door, so as to be ready for anything that may be inside. He counts to three in his head, grabs the handle again and swings the door open.

Kevin M. Moehring

Chapter 8

Stuart has been shining the flashlight from side to side and every step he takes brings about a new set of park signs and various places that someone could be hiding. In all the years of being a police officer in Twisted Timbers, he has never felt so scared. Now he finds himself all alone in a dark, closed amusement park, looking for whomever is supposedly hanging around. Even though he isn't really sure there is anyone at all.

All the rides in the kiddie area are highlighted with bright colors and happy characters. During the daylight hours the faces of clowns, animals and other kid friendly characters are an inviting sight for the hordes of kids that visit the park. As he walks through the area, Stuart thinks that Mitch sent him here as a joke. Another way of making fun of him for his lack of courage. Knowing these faces would make the hairs on his arms stand up, as they are currently doing.

He has just about made his way through the last of the rides in the area. Along the way, he tripped over one of the bumper cars, his rifle handle got caught on the gate when he tried to get a closer look at the helicopter ride and now he is making his way toward the carousel. Other than the Ferris Wheel, the carousel is the most often talked about ride in all of Graham Park. It dates back to the late 1800's and every piece is hand crafted. The horses, giraffes and elephants have all been hand painted and even the music the ride plays is original. Even when he would ride the carousel as a child, he often thought the faces on the animals were creepy and gave him goosebumps.

Stuart takes up position behind the nearest park bench and uses his light to get an unobstructed view of the carousel. He wants to make sure the coast is clear before he proceeds. In his mind he can see the creepy faces of the animals coming to life and jumping off of the carousel and charging at him. None of this is actually going to happen but Stuart is a firm believer in the better safe than sorry philosophy. From where he is positioned the darkness makes it hard to make out any exact details on the ride but there doesn't appear to be anything in the vicinity that could harm him.

He leaves the safety and comfort that the park bench had temporarily provided and heads for the carousel. Without the bright lights and the music playing, Stuart can't help but notice the ride is showing the effects of years spent battling the elements. There are dozens of areas where the paint is peeling away. He wonders to himself if it is part of the annual routine to repaint each and every horse, to keep their faces smiling and new. Several of the boards that support the horses have begun to creek and show signs of warping. Much to his delight he has found nothing unusual with any of the animals he has looked at so far.

Without thinking about it he starts to hum the unforgettable calypso tune that he remembers the ride would play repeatedly. Now that he has seen nothing to report back to Mitch about, he has lowered his level of alert and has begun to relax. Around the back side of the ride is the door that allows the mechanics to enter the center of the ride, to do repairs if needed. The outside walls of the center room are all decorated with mirrors that have been framed in ornate wood carvings. The door appears to the riders as if it is just another wall or another mirror but as Stuart shines his light in that general direction, he can see that the door is slightly ajar.

Stuart is quick to pull the rifle back around in front of his body. This was not what he wanted to have happen in the least. Maybe the door was left open at the end of last season, but he is not willing to take any chances. He tucks the flashlight under his arm and uses the tip of his weapon to open the door further. As he begins to shine the light into the opening, his feet become tangled in something and he loses his balance. He shines the light to the floor and sees a tangle of thick ropes that are now wrapped around his ankles.

Once he wiggles his feet free, he can see that one end of the ropes is tied to large poles inside the small room that holds the mechanical parts that allow the ride to function. He drops all of the ropes except for one and follows it to find out where it leads. The rope snakes its way through several horses until it hangs loosely around the neck of a pink horse that is in mid-gallop. The knot holding the rope around the porcelain horse is extensive and tied tightly. Stuart follows the rope back to the open door and grabs another rope. This one leads him to a bright orange tiger that looks like he is about to take a bite out of his prey with his bright white teeth. Again, the rope is wrapped around the animal, in the area where the rider would sit, on top of the back of the tiger.

Stuart stands motionless for a moment trying to figure out the significance of these ropes and studies the intricacy with which each of the knots are tied. These ropes must have been tied like this for a reason, someone obviously took time to master the knots perfectly. The opening on the ends look large enough that they could be used to tie down a large animal or even a person. There has to be some kind of logical explanation for the ropes being attached to the center of the ride. If the ride were to turn on, these ropes would surely do damage of some sort. Either they would pull the porcelain animals they were attached to right out of the warped boards that they are bolted down to or there would be considerable damage to the inner workings of the ride itself.

He is standing there in what is usually a very happy spot for children, completely perplexed by the significance of what he has found. He is brought back to reality by a large popping sound. At first, the sound doesn't trigger any feeling of panic in him. Moments later he hears the sound again, followed by a sizable portion of the tiger's ear flying past his head. His mind is racing now and after a few rapid heartbeats, his senses tell him that he needs to move. Stuart practically throws his body into the small opening behind the mirrored door and slams it shut behind him. His heart is pounding, and he is out of breath. He rights himself and searches his pocket for his radio, but it is nowhere to be found. As he thinks back on the events that occurred since he left Mitch, when they all did a radio check, he thinks there could be many places he could have dropped his radio.

He uses the flashlight to become better acquainted with the tight space he is now forced to occupy. There isn't much room to maneuver, which would have made it hard for the mechanics to do any kind of repair that would have been needed. With some slight contorting, he is able to position his body so that his back is resting on a large panel that holds electrical wires, which allows him to sit in the prone position with his rifle pointing at the door. As his muscles become tenser, he fears that he will not be able to leave his current location. The fact that there is apparently someone outside taking shots at him reinforces his theory that he will be much safer if he stays put, with his finger on the trigger. A finger that is connected to a hand that is now trembling with a sweaty palm. He is frozen in place, content to wait out whatever is happening on the outside, in the somewhat safety of the tiny room.

Chapter 9

Fred Donovan has always been quick to prove that he's

a man. He has a reputation around town of taking his job a little too seriously. He seems to always turn even the smallest of confrontations into something much larger than it needs to be. He loves his job, mostly because he yearns for the respect and added attention that comes along with wearing the badge. Often times he uses the squad car and the police station as props to try and convince the single women of Twisted Timbers into going out with him. Rarely does it work.

As he strolls through the walkways of the water park, which has been dubbed Old Mill Country, he whistles the tune to an old country song his mother would often sing to him. There has been nothing remarkable to see in this part of the park and his radio has remained silent. Fred walked quickly through the various playgrounds that have water nozzles that spray the young guests with water to cool them off on the hot summer days. He practically ran through the entire length of the log flume which looked promising when he embarked but ended up providing nothing but large spider webs. The wooden channel that normally holds gallons of water and ushers a cart full of passengers up and down hills, sounded like it could fall apart at any moment under the weight of his steps.

Fred was anxious to get through his area and find anything that would lead them in the right direction. He longs for the attention that comes along with being the person to solve the case. He is now making his way to the section of Old Mill Country that is furthest away from the parking lot and the Ferris Wheel. There is a various assortment of water slides in this portion of the park. Fred takes the stairs of the first slide two at a time and reaches the top in what he considers must be record time. He takes a moment to look around from atop the slide. He can almost make out the Nehalem River from this position and the strokes of lightning that have been decorating the night sky add to the view. Other than the Ferris Wheel and the roller coaster, this slide is the highest point in all of Graham Park. He can see over almost all of the trees and sees the storm getting closer.

Moments later he hears a single gunshot which pierces through the night air. It would be hard to tell the difference between the sounds of the storm and the faint shot off in the distance if Fred wasn't an avid hunter. Seconds later he hears another shot and while his eyes are fixed on the horizon and the surrounding areas, he is almost certain he was able to make out the sight of a muzzle flash from on top of the roller coaster.

As more lightning claps behind him, he becomes more certain that the two sounds he heard were not lightning. At first, he is irritated that he was not in the right place to be the first to get some action. He doesn't even give a moment's thought to the safety or well-being of his fellow officers. Fred wants to get to the action quickly and lowers his body into the dry tube and heads down the slide. The ride is a bit rougher without the water that would normally be gushing. Like a load of wrinkled laundry, he empties out onto the hard surface of the small concrete pool at the bottom. He quickly jumps to his feet and takes off in a sprint, heading to the area where the three men were supposed to meet after they had finished their individual searches.

The sprint gets the better of him more quickly than he would like to admit, and his body forces him to stop and catch his breath. He decides to run back toward the front gate along a different route than he took to get to the water park. This route will take him through the intersection where the midway gives way to the front entrance of the only roller coaster that can be found at Graham Park. He stops long enough to look toward the coaster for any sign that Mitch is in the area. Failing to see him he takes off in a light jog down the midway toward the Ferris Wheel. It isn't long until his fear over hearing the gun shots is replaced with confusion over what he is seeing in front of him.

About halfway down the midway, in between where there would normally be dozens of carnival games, there is a bright light coming out of a structure that resembles a hut. As he nears the structure he is relieved to see that his flashlight is no longer needed. He turns it off, sticks it in the appropriate holster in his belt and returns his rifle to the front side of his body. His stride has slowed as he nears the rear of the building and can see the door is wide open.

He follows the light that leads the way in front of him, sticks the barrel of rifle into the room first, then leaps in with a scream. As much as he likes to come off as a tough guy, his heart is beating out of his chest. The room is tiny, with nowhere for anyone to hide. This is obviously a building that is normally used to sell food and drinks to the guests. There are stacks of soda cups lined on the overhead shelving. In the corner of the room is a large lantern that is burning brightly. It is not uncommon in this part of the world to find a lantern like this. Camping is the primary leisure activity of anyone who lives in the northwest. Finding one burning in this hut, however, is highly peculiar.

In an attempt to be thorough, Fred grabs the handle of the lantern and turns around the room. The walls feel like they are right on top of him. There is barely enough room for him to stand in place and turn completely around without knocking things off of the shelves. There isn't much in the room and Fred decides this is a safe place to use his radio and ask the other two guys how they are doing. He waits several minutes but no replies come over the radio. He reaches outside and grabs the handle of the door and closes it tight. This is the first time he is seeing the inside of the door because when he swung it open he was more focused on what was inside of the room instead of anything affixed to the inside of the door itself.

From top to bottom the door is covered with blue prints of the park and other papers which have been secured with tape. Every ride, every building, even every electrical panel is systematically drawn out in great detail. There must be a dozen or so schematics on this door Fred thinks to himself. He quickly reaches for his cell phone and notices he has zero service, as is not uncommon this far away from town and in the middle of the woods. He doesn't intend to make any phone calls but rather snap pictures of everything on the door that he has found so he can show them to Mitch, or better yet, the sheriff.

Chapter 10

Mitch didn't know which way he was running in the moments following the gun shots. All he knew is that he was running in the general direction from which he thought he heard the sound. His body is moving faster than it has since high school and the fact that he has needed to stop and catch his breath makes him feel like he is a teenager again. It didn't take long for him to see there wasn't much to be found in the small hut building except for a camping lantern but when the shots rang out, he knew he needed to get moving.

His first reaction was to take cover, but it didn't take long for him to realize that the shots came from far enough away that he was in no real danger. Judging by the direction of the shots, his best guess is that they came from the south, and not far from where he had sent Stuart to investigate. Mitch forgets about the lantern and the contents of the small hut and takes off in the direction of the roller coaster in a panic. He is moving so fast that he finds it difficult to use the radio properly, fumbles with it for a second, before it falls to the hard concrete below his feet. He doubles back and snatches it up with a less than graceful dip before once again sprinting ahead.

It takes him just a few minutes to reach the area just outside of the roller coaster. The ride is called The Log Splitter and a devious face of a deranged clown marks the entrance for visitors. Even in the day time this vision is unwelcoming, but now in the dark of night, it is even more creepy. He has ridden this ride on numerous occasions over the years and can still remember the big steep hills and the sharply banked curves of the wooden structure. He has never been able to figure out exactly what the face on the sign was meant to represent. The smiling mouth with bloody fangs, the dark eyes clashing with the bright red cheeks. It never really made that much sense to him, but it definitely worked at intimidating the riders.

He grabs his radio once more and is devastated to see that the small light that lets you know that it is operating properly is no longer lit. In his haste he dropped it and the force of it hitting the concrete has left a big crack on the side. He slams the unit down to the ground in a furious rage. Was he too eager to prove to his father that he could handle whatever is going on in here? His own heartbeat is ringing through his body, causing him to sweat profusely. The sounds of the impending storm fill the void left by his panting and he desperately yells for either of his co-workers to respond to his voice. No response from either man. He inches his way along the concrete path which winds through a maze of metal railings and heads toward the passenger loading area for the ride. He is making sure that his footsteps fall silent on the ground, which is far easier to do now than it usually is on his hunting trips in the woods.

With his flashlight leading the way he makes his way along the path, through the twisting poles of metal. He never really remembered the line being this long before but maybe it just seems longer due to the current circumstances. Every few steps he stops long enough to listen to his surroundings. Once he is certain he is alone, he yells out again for Stuart or Fred, when in reality if anyone at all could hear him it would settle his nerves. A few more steps and he makes it to the front of the ride, where passengers line up in pairs and get seated in their corresponding cars for the ride.

Mitch stands for a long moment trying to figure out what he is looking at. When he reached the boarding area, he expected to see a row of empty passenger cars but instead his eyes are drawn to the very first car in the row. He quickly shines the flashlight around the area on the opposite side of the track, just to make sure he is alone. A few steps to his left and he is now standing in front of the first car. When he first laid eyes on it, Mitch wasn't quite sure what he was looking at. Now, as he stands about three feet away and from an angle which allows him to look down into the seat, he sees a large body, bound by thick chains. The chains are wrapped around the torso, through the handle and leg restraint that is all that usually keeps the passengers from flying out on the long downhills portions. The body is sitting much higher in the chair than a normal rider would be, resting on what looks to be a large wooden box.

Above the chains, much of the shirt that covers the chest of the body is covered in blood. He rubs a couple of fingers across the body and the blood is thick and sticky. The accident that caused this blood obviously happened not long ago, the blood is less viscous and warmer than it would be if the wound was days old. The arms of the body are bound tightly behind the back, but the posture is preventing Mitch from seeing what is keeping them back there.

Between the torrential downpours that are frequent in this part of the country and the winding, hilly roads in the area, Mitch has seen his fair share of bloody accident scenes. What he has just walked up on in the seating area of *The Wood Splitter* is different in one very glaring way. The victim that he is looking at here is missing one thing that makes it hard for Mitch to look at the body without feeling sick to his stomach. The body that is secured in the passenger car is lacking any sign that a head was at one time connected to the body.

Kevin M. Moehring

Chapter 11

Stuart is content with his hiding spot although he is quickly becoming claustrophobic. Being crammed in such a tiny space for so long is starting to play tricks on his mind. He does regret the fact that he lost his radio somewhere along the way and even more frustrated with the lack of service he gets every time he checks his cell phone. He has remained squatted in this tiny space with his finger on the trigger of his rifle for what seems like hours. He knows from the clock on his phone that it has only been about twenty minutes since he heard the shots.

Beads of sweat drip down his face and land on the barrel of the rifle. He fears that if he was actually forced to fire the rifle in this area, he would most certainly go deaf from the concussion. Luckily, up to this point, he has heard no sounds outside of the mirrored door that shields him from the animals of the carousel and whoever it is that has decided to treat him as target practice. He is well aware of his reputation around town of being the most scared officer in the history of law enforcement. With a gunman on the loose in Graham Park, there is nowhere that Stuart would rather be than in this small room with only one way in, which he is guarding with his rifle.

A quick check of the cell phone again, it's now been twenty-six minutes since he fled for cover. Another attempt to reach Mitch and another failed connection. As he slides his phone back into his jeans pocket, he is suddenly hit with the urge to urinate. Stuart has been told for years that drinking too much coffee would be the death of him and now he's starting to think everyone was right.

He uses his back to push his body up until he is standing on his feet once again. The room is so small that the rifle is pressed against his chest now and his nose is face to face with the inside of the door. He remains motionless for a split second until he loses his balance as the entire floor he is standing on begins to rotate. What was once a silent darkness is now well lit and filled with the very loud tones of the usually joyful music that plays while the ride is in motion. He can hear the gears turning behind him, causing the poles on the outside to lift the horses and other animals as they spin around.

If the eerie silence was playing on his nerves, the noise that echoes against the walls of the tiny space is enough to drive him mad. He knows that more than likely the only way to start the ride is from the control panel where the ride operator usually sits, meaning someone is probably waiting for him once he opens the door. The floor moves faster and faster, quicker than Stuart can ever remember it going when he was a child. Is this the result of being in the middle of the ride or has whoever turned the ride on somehow been able to manipulate the speed?

Soon after contemplating the likelihood that someone was able to turn up the power of the gears, his thoughts are interrupted as his body goes into a coughing fit. The coughs are deep and bellowing, resembling that of a man who has smoked for most of his life, unlike Stuart. A quick look around and a cloud of smoke rushes at his eyes and into his face, causing him to drop his rifle and flashlight and rub furiously at his eyes. He blindly reaches for the handle to the door, opens it and stumbles out of the room. He manages to collapse across the back of a zebra, which appears to be one of the only animals on the ride that doesn't go up and down.

Now that he is out of the room and away from the smoke, he is able to rub enough of the black soot from his eyes to allow his vision to return. What was once just a dark collection of fake animals, is now lit up brightly and rotating around in record speed. The ride is moving so fast that it causes the bright colors to all bleed together into a blurry rainbow. Even without his flashlight, Stuart is able to quickly find the control panel that operates the ride. He looks down on it without the slightest idea of what any of the knobs or switches actually does. He starts turning things at random, but nothing has any effect on the ride. A turn of the red knob, a tug on the black switch, a push of the yellow button. Nothing he does will stop the ride or the annoying music that now seems to be melodically making fun of him.

Out of aggravation he gives the pedestal that holds the control panel a strong kick. A glimpse of light reflects from something on the underside of the panel and catches his eye. He drops to his knees to find a key protruding from the underside of the metal panel. He turns the key quickly and pulls it out from the machine.

Instantly the ride begins to slow, and the music tapers off until the silence is returned. Stuart rushes back to the door from where he escaped and grabs his rifle and his flashlight.

Now that the ride has been shut down and the lights have once again gone dark, his flashlight leads the way as he walks through the animals looking for the ropes he found before he heard the shots. They are nowhere to be found. He finds the tiger that lost his ear to the second shot, walks completely around the carousel until he returns to the same damaged animal again. Still, he was unable to find any ropes that are tied to animals, just a few fragments hanging out below the mirrored door, that are frayed at the end. Someone has obviously been here and cut the ropes and they were really close to him when he was hiding in the room.

Once again, he pulls out his phone to check for service and returns it to his pocket with the same feeling of loneliness. A quick shine of the flashlight behind him and he wonders if it's worth the effort, or even if it's safe, for him to go hunting for the radio he lost. For a second he thinks he catches something in the mirror on the wall on the inside of the carousel. A quick turn on his heels with the flashlight still leading the way reveals that there is nothing there. Stuart stares at his own reflection in the mirror for a while, hating himself for being so scared. The top of his uniform is no longer tucked in properly and he knows if the sheriff were to see him in this condition, Sheriff Thompson would make some sort of snide remark. Stuart throws the rifle over his shoulder and tucks his flashlight under his arm. He didn't mean to do it but the fact that he pointed the beam of light away from the mirror revealed to him what caught his eye in the first place.

He stops tucking his shirt in long enough to read the message on the mirror. After shining his light on the reflective glass again, it's apparent that the message is written in some kind of glowing ink that disappears when it is seen in the light. Once the meaning of the message sinks in, Stuart drops his flashlight. His knees are shaking, and his hands are trembling as he reads the words out loud in an effort to memorize them, so he can repeat them to the others if he ever sees them again.

With the events that just happened, even the sound of his own voice sends chills down his body. The ink used to write the message appears as bright yellow and must have been very wet when it was written. Some of the ink has run down the mirror and makes some of the words harder to read than others. He reads them aloud for a third time, this time he lets each word linger in the air before reading the next. He has always had trouble remembering key facts about the cases he has dealt with in the past but there is no chance he will forget these words any time soon. They essentially put a bounty on his head, and the heads of his fellow officers.

Kevin M. Moehring

Chapter 12

Among the numerous schematics and maps that are posted on the inside of the door, Fred finds a list of six names. Next to the name of each person is a small black and white picture with a short bio. Most of the names are hard to pronounce for him, meaning they are more than likely foreign. The info that is listed lets him know that each man is currently, or has been in the past, a member of the military in whatever country they come from.

On the large map of the park, the one that shows every ride and location of every path that is not intended to be used by the paying public, there is a series of lines that have been drawn in red ink. Each of these lines starts at the carousel and ends with a large circle drawn around another aspect of the park. One leads to the roller coaster, another to the water park, a third to the kids rides and a final one, which has the biggest circle, ends at the Ferris Wheel.

The rest of the papers affixed to the wall are much more confusing to Fred. One appears to be the wiring schematics for the entire park. Maybe this is how someone was able to turn on the Ferris Wheel without having to contact the power company to restore the electricity to the park. He looks at most of the items with a look of confusion, not being able to decipher the words that are written on them. Either the words are too complicated for him or they are not in a language that he understands.

At the bottom of the door, almost hidden behind the large map of Graham Park, he finds a small note with some peculiar listings. At the heading of the sheet of loose leaf paper is the title: 'Rewards for souvenirs' written in black marker. Underneath the title there are several things listed in a column on the right-hand side of the paper, with a corresponding number amount on the left. Fred looks over the list and is frightened by what he sees. Even though he doesn't know the meaning of any of the information, he is frightened to find out that a head in a box is worth fifty grand according to this list. There is a dollar amount listed for almost every body part, ten grand for hands, feet and genitalia, twenty-five thousand for eyes or tongue and a hundred thousand for the heart.

The small piece of paper puts a far more serious tone to the rest of the things hanging from the door. Many of have them could have been explained in a manner that made everyone feel safe that nothing odd was happening. Now that he has found a price list for body parts, to go along with the list of names and faces, it makes even the normally macho Fred feel like a school kid who is about to enter his first haunted house.

He tears down the three pages that he wants to take along with him, the list of names, the pricing sheet and most importantly the map of the park with the lines drawn out. He folds them all neatly and stuffs them into his pocket. A few unanswered calls on the radio, a quick check of his cell phone for service and another check of the ammo in his rifle later, he closes the door to the hut and leaves the lantern inside. He would love to bring it with him, but it is far too cumbersome to try to carry it and still be able to use his rifle.

Since every line on the map originated from the large square that was drawn around the carousel, he heads in that direction. His stride is a little more hesitant after finding the information on the inside of the door. When he first set off to investigate the water park, he was almost skipping along. Now Fred is covering the distance to the carousel in a hectic pattern that includes hiding behind a large garbage can, diving headfirst behind a row of overgrown shrubs and sliding underneath a large park bench. He is not sure that all of the extra precautions are necessary but in his own mind his motions are as fluid and graceful as anyone he has ever seen in the movies.

With the carousel in sight his pace slows further. He is bent at the knees and moving as if his next step could trigger an invisible land mine, another technique he learned from the movies. As he passes the last obstacle before reaching the ride, a wooden structure that was used to sell soft-serve ice cream, the ride starts up. He retreats to the front-side of the building he is next to and presses his back up against the large piece of plywood that protects the glass windows from the hard winter. He listens intently trying to hear footsteps on the concrete but the music from the ride is loud enough that he probably wouldn't even hear another gunshot if there was one.

With a slight bend of the neck he peeks his head around the corner of the ice cream building. The lights of the carousel are bright, flashing whites, yellows and oranges pierce through the darkness and cause Fred to squint slightly. The animals on the ride are bouncing up and down and beginning to go around and round much faster than normal. Returning to the safety of the opposite side of the building, once again he checks the ammo in his rifle. Confident it is loaded properly, he lowers his body, spins on his heels and takes up a comfortable position with the barrel pointed at the ride. From this position he can cover both sides of the carousel and would be able to move the rifle with ease to point it at a potential target.

He peers down the barrel of the weapon, the cold steel pressed against his cheek, waiting to catch a glimpse of the person responsible for turning on the machine. The ride is spinning at such a rapid pace that it is hard to make out the animals individually as they pass by. Moments later a dark puff of smoke can be seen from the center of the ride, followed closely by a dark figure. It is nearly impossible to make out any distinguishing features on the figure, but he follows the person closely as they stumble through the animals and disappears behind the ride.

The rotating lights are somewhat hypnotizing to Fred as the colors swirl around. The fact that there is something very strange going on and for a second he thought the carousel was going to go up in a cloud of smoke, is lost on Fred. The calypso music, the flashing lights and the porcelain animals going up and down has forced a momentary lapse in judgement and caused him to let his guard down. The barrel of the rifle is no longer pointed at the ride and has fallen harmlessly to the concrete walkway, near where he is kneeling.

Seconds later the music begins to slow, as does the ride itself. Fred snaps back to the reality that someone turned on the ride and someone else came stumbling out from the room inside. One of the two could very easily be the person responsible for the shots he heard while he was on top of the water slide. He assumes the shooting position once more and focuses his sights on the door on the inside of the ride, the one where the dark figure escaped from.

Now that the ride is slowing, he can start to make out the brightly painted animals that pass in front of him one by one. The music that fills the air now reminds Fred of his father's old records that he would play at the wrong speed, each note dragging out multiple beats longer than it should. Once the ride comes to a complete stop, he has a line of sight on three sides of it, but the door to the room stopped on the opposite side and is hidden to him.

Other than the brief initial sighting, he has not been able to locate the person than came rushing out of the interior room. He has no idea as to who is responsible for turning on the ride in the first place, as he was never able to get a visual on them either. Deciding that he needs to move forward so he can inspect the other side of the ride and the doorway, he stands to his feet. Fred pays close attention to the barrel of the rifle, making certain that it remains pointed in the direction of the ride. Once to his feet he is once again thrown off-guard, this time by a tap on his shoulder.

Kevin M. Moehring

Chapter 13

Unlike most people, Mitch Thompson is not disgusted by finding a headless body chained down in the front seat of the roller coaster train. Instead, he reacts as any police officer would. His eyes scan the immediate area looking for any clues that could be laying around, he takes out his phone and snaps pictures of the body from every angle and he jots down the time that he arrived on the scene and found the body. All of this would be standard protocol in a situation like this, which would be a much more common occurrence in a large city like Portland or Seattle. In Twisted Timbers, especially during the off-season, this is a much bigger find than Mitch is used to. He can't even remember the last time he even heard about a murder in the small town.

Now he stands in front of a decapitated body, trying to determine if it's a smart move to search the victim for any evidence. He knows that his father would frown upon touching the body, he preaches preserving a crime scene any chance he gets, but this is an active crime scene. Any and all information could be crucial to understanding what is going on in the park and might help Mitch determine what course of action to take as the night proceeds.

Considering the current circumstances, the wrath of his father fails in comparison to ending up like the body in the roller coaster car. It's hard for Mitch to get his hands into the jeans pocket that the victim was wearing when he was killed. The positioning of the body has forced the entire weight of the torso to tighten the jeans in the area where the hips bend. After a bit of a struggle, which requires him to lower his weapon and leave it to rest on the side of the passenger car, he can reach down inside all the pockets of the victim.

There is no wallet or identification of any kind. In fact, there wasn't much inside the pockets at all. He pulled out a single folded piece of paper, a couple of shotgun shells and a utility knife. He leaves the shells and the knife on top of the lap of the victim, the identity of the man still a mystery to him. He unfolds the sheet of paper to find a list of six names and faces. Each picture is followed by an array of factual information regarding the person, including military rank and country of origin. On the reverse side of the paper there is a typed-out form, consisting of numbered lines of text that cover the entire length of the page, all below a heading that reads *'The Rules of the Game'*.

Mitch is somewhat relieved to read the first rule of the game as it is listed on the paper. It states that the game will officially begin once the lights of the Ferris Wheel go out. Now he can show this to the other two officers and they will know that he was not crazy when he called in the initial sighting of the ride in operation. The last rule says that all players were to be start out on the carousel and could not begin the hunt until after the lights went out on the Ferris Wheel. He quickly scans the rest of the rules, none of which really make sense to him, and begins to fold the paper back to how it was when he found it in the pocket of his victim.

Once the note is safely in the outside shirt pocket of his police uniform, Mitch once again looks behind him to make sure he is alone. There is nobody else on the ride platform, but he can now see another part of the park is lit up. He uses the scope on his rifle to get a closer look.

He raises the rifle to his left eye, closes his right eye and stares at the carousel that is functionally fully at this point. The animals are spinning around and around, and Mitch can hear the celebratory music playing in the distance.

Without thinking twice about it, he takes off in a dead sprint in the general direction of the carousel, hoping to get there long before any of the people responsible for the operation of the ride are able to flee the area. A long hurdle of the exit gate to the roller coaster allows him to reach the ramp that leads the exiting passengers back onto the midway of the park. Instead of heading back to the front of the park and taking the path that cuts between the carnival games, Mitch decides that jumping the fence and taking a direct path through the trees would be faster. The thickness of the trees and overgrown shrubs make the trek more difficult than he first thought but the music of the carousel is getting louder and louder, so he continues on. Once he gets close enough, the lights from the ride make the task of making his way through the low hanging branches much easier.

Another tall chain link fence, covered in vines, blocks his path to the carousel. Mitch stands well over six feet tall and is able to cross the fence with relative ease. Once he is on the other side, he turns his attention to the music that's playing and the ride that is spinning. To the left of the ride is an ice cream stand that has been secured for the winter months by covering the windows with sheets of plywood. Behind the building he can also make out a shadow and judging from what he can see, it looks like the person is holding a rifle.

Mitch retreats backwards until his back is flush against the fence. He bumps it harder than he would have liked, and the metal makes a ringing sound that he hopes was quiet enough so that the shadow person was unable to hear it. As if on cue, as soon as Mitch raises the rifle to look through the scope, the ride begins to slow. He turns the rifle in the direction of the ride and catches another glimpse of a figure stumbling off the ride to the rear. Smoke is now hovering above the ride and is streaming out of the center as if the entire ride would soon go up in a ball of flames.

Another sound off to his right distracts him from the falling figure and the black smoke. His reaction is too slow to catch any sight of the person that caused the sound and if it wasn't for the rustling of a few branches, Mitch wouldn't even have been certain that he heard anything at all. With the area around him covered in darkness once again, thanks to the ride slowly shutting down, Mitch becomes more daring and heads toward the back of the ice cream building. The person who is hiding on the opposite side is now on one knee, with his rifle pointed toward the now quiet ride. The relief rushes over him the moment he realizes that this shadowy figure is someone he knows. He walks faster than he would if he were trying to sneak up on someone, not caring if the person less than a few feet in front of him can hear him. Mitch retreats a few feet when he taps Fred on the shoulder and the normally brave officer let's out a squeal reminiscent of an elementary school girl.

"Holy shit Mitch, you almost gave me a heart attack." As much as Mitch is happy to see Fred, it fails in comparison to the happiness in the older officer's voice. Fred had hoped to be the person to break the case wide open, now that there is obviously more going on at Graham Park than he bargained for, he is relieved to have a partner. "Why didn't you use your radio? Have you heard from Stuart?"

Mitch steps closer to Fred and places his finger over his own mouth, the universal symbol to lower your voice. "I dropped my radio when I took off running toward the roller coaster after I heard the shots." If you were not standing right next to him, you would never be able to hear the words that are coming out of his mouth. Fred nods when he hears that Mitch also heard the shots earlier. "I have not heard from Stuart, I was kind of hoping that you knew where he was. I don't think we're alone here. I found this paper that has a list of what I would describe as very bad men. Every one of them are former military guys and I don't think they are here to enjoy the scenery of our great town."

Fred reaches into his chest pocket and pulls out a stack of folded papers of his own. "I found a few things too, are these the same people that are listed on your paper?"

Mitch gives a folded piece of crumbled paper a quick look, nods his head and starts to fold his paper back up. "Where did you find that and what's on the other papers?"

Fred kneels down in front of Mitch, lays out the three pieces of paper across the cement in between them.

"I found them all taped to the door of the small beverage hut in the middle of the midway. I ran that direction when I heard the shots. There was a lit lantern in there too, meaning someone had been there recently."

"I found the room too and the lantern was lit when I got there. I didn't have much time to look around because when I heard the shots I took off." He adds extra emphasis on the last line in hopes that Fred would not read too much into the fact that Mitch could have left valuable evidence behind. "I see the list of names and faces and that looks to be a map of the park. I can't make out what's on the small piece, I never learned how to read upside down."

Fred grabs the smallest scrap of paper and turns it toward Mitch. "I'm not sure what it is exactly but it looked important enough for me to snatch it off of the door. It's a list of body parts, followed by a corresponding dollar amount for each. It looks like someone has organized some sort of game where body parts are traded for large amounts of cash."

"That would help explain something," Mitch looks long and hard at the sheet of paper, before returning it to the neatly laid out design that Fred has created.

"Explain something? What do you mean?" Fred looks up at Mitch like a kid who is waiting eagerly for his father to teach him about the facts of life.

"When I got to the roller coaster I found a body in the front car of the train. I searched the body for any identification and that's when I found my copy of the name list." Mitch shakes the piece of paper in his hand for emphasis.

"So, there is definitely something not right happening here, but that still doesn't help me understand why this list of body parts and dollar amounts helps to explain anything. "Again, Fred looks at his colleague with anticipation. While he might be the bravest of all of the police officers in Twisted Timbers, he will never be labeled as the smartest.

"When I first walked up to the passenger car, I didn't really know what I was looking at. The body had hands bound behind him at the waist and there was a ton of blood. The list of body parts you have here, combined with the list of rules on the back of my paper, help me figure out what is going on. By looking at the list of price amounts, it appears to me that the person responsible for killing the man in the roller coaster car is now fifty grand richer."

It takes a while for Fred to catch on to what he is being told. When it finally sinks in, he snatches the paper from the ground, looks down at the column of dollar amounts, finds the row that shows fifty thousand and uses his pointer finger to direct his eyes to the matching body part. "Oh, hell no! The body in the roller coaster is missing a head?"

Chapter 14

Stuart stands motionless, staring at the words written on the mirror, trying to understand the meaning of the message. The first line is a simple single word, written in letters much larger than the rest. The word *CREW* spelled out in all caps at the top of the mirror is obviously intended to grab the attention of a group or pack of people. The following sentences are intended to inform the so-called crew that there are three new players in the game and that the head of each one is worth seventy-five grand.

Stuart remains frozen in place, staring at the mirror, trying to figure out what is causing him the most fear. On one hand, the fact that the ride started while he was inside is a strong indication that someone knew he was in there and was a few steps away from him without him even knowing it. On the other hand, the last line of the message on the mirror clearly points a finger at himself and his two fellow officers. The last word in the message, again written in all caps, is *LAW*. There is no doubt in his mind that this refers to the fact that the three people in the park wearing badges are now a part of some sort of game and that the killing of any of the three officers would earn someone thousands of dollars.

Suddenly Stuart Johnson has the feeling as if someone is watching him, spins around and shines his flashlight into the trees behind him. His heart rate has not slowed one bit since the ride started up unexpectedly. With his rifle barrel shaking, matching the motions of the flashlight, he searches the tree covered area behind him. He doesn't know he is doing it but with every swipe of the flashlight from side to side, Stuart takes a small step away from the woods and closer to the carousel. In typical Stuart fashion, it isn't long before he trips over the ledge of the carousel and falls backward. He ends up under the back legs of a giraffe, looking up at the gold painted stirrups. The commotion must have startled someone on the other side of the ride because as soon as he hit the ground he heard a feminine sounding gasp from that direction. He quickly rolls to his stomach, he has gotten very good at trying to disguise his clumsiness over the years. He makes his way to the opposite side of the ride, dodging the animals one by one as if he were on a tour at some kind of crazy taxidermy safari.

Once on the opposite side of the carousel, he uses the bent leg of a white horse to steady his rifle and aims it near the area where he heard the sound. There's an ice cream stand in the middle of the walkway and from this angle he can see a slight beam of light in the space between the building and the fence behind it. His hands instantly start to tremble, his rifle is no longer secure on the leg of the animal and begins to make clanking sounds as the cold metal of the barrel taps against the gold buckles of the reigns on the brightly painted horse.

For the third time in the last hour, Stuart is frozen in place. This time he is certain there is someone just steps away from him and his life is most certainly in danger. This is the first time he has ever thought that his mother was right when she told him that becoming a police officer would be a bad career choice. From deep in his throat he feels a tickle building. It comes on slowly at first but the black smoke he ingested has made fighting off the cough an exercise in futility. In the brief moment before the cough hits, Stuart wonders if anyone has ever been killed as a direct result from coughing.

"Stuart, is that you?" The voice calls out from behind the ice cream stand soon after the sound of the cough subsides. He is so happy to hear a voice that he recognizes that he almost forgets to respond.

"Mitch, are you back there? I am so glad you're here." He waits until Mitch steps out from behind the ice cream stand, followed closely behind by Fred. Stuart practically jumps up from his crouch and leaps from the ledge of the ride like any one of the thousands of young kids who rode this very ride in the past. "Come over here, you have to see what I found written on this mirror."

Mitch and Fred walk side by side toward Stuart, as he happily strides closer to them. His heartbeat has finally slowed to a much more normal rhythm. He no longer fears that he will die alone on a kid's ride in an amusement park. His fellow officers have shown up and the three of them together will surely be a much more intimidating force than Stuart cowering in the corner alone. As he approaches the other two men his overwhelming feeling of relief is taken over by excruciating pain running through his leg. It's not that he didn't hear the shot come from behind him as much as it was that the instantaneous feeling of pain over-powered his senses. He drops his flashlight and rifle, as his body crumbles to the ground in a heap. The last thing he sees before he passes out is the back of Mitch, as he runs away and disappears behind the building.

Kevin M. Moehring

Chapter 15

With his five-year advantage in age, Mitch is easily able to beat Fred to the rear of the snack building. They both retreated as quickly as possible after hearing the gun shot and had their backs turned well before their fellow officer crumbled to the ground. The two men dove head first behind the safety of the wooden walls, a collection of legs and arms flying through the air that was surely a spectacle to watch. As they untangle themselves, their attention turns to their fallen partner.

Mitch takes control of the situation and is the first to be gutsy enough to stick his head around the corner of the building to check on his friend. Stuart is about fifty yards away from the back side of the building. He lays motionless on the cold ground, his hands out to his side as if he were making snow angles. He is obviously too far away for Mitch to be able to tell if the man is still breathing.

"Did you see where it hit him?" There is a long silence before Mitch returns his head to safety and looks at Fred. "I heard the shot and took off running, were you able to see where it hit Stu?"

Fred returns the question with a shake of the head. It's easy to see that his body is tense, and fear has almost taken him over. He stares straight ahead of him, which causes Mitch to look in the same direction. There is nothing there except a fence, trees and bushes in dire need of trimming.

"Fred, I need you to focus. This is not the time for you to be freezing up on me." The fact that the officer who has long been considered the bravest of them all is having a panic attack is not a good sign for the safety of the men. "We have to get Stuart out of there. If he is still alive, he won't be for long unless we go and get him." Mitch places his hand on the forearm of his fellow officer, squeezing slightly to show him that he has the situation under control.

"You think he's still alive?" Apparently, this notion never crossed his mind and hearing the words out loud brings him back into reality. "I guess he could be, huh? I didn't see where the shot hit him. Is he moving?"

"He's too far away. I can't even tell if he's breathing. All I know is, even if he is dead, we are not leaving him out there alone. Lord knows what these people will do to him, they obviously have a fetish for body parts."

"Damn it Mitch, don't talk like that!" Fred is normally a very laid-back individual but after seeing his friend get shot, he is unable to play the role any longer. "What do you suggest we do? If the guy who is taking shots is one of the guys on that paper, then we are dealing with a professional."

Mitch takes a few seconds to scout the area, looking on all sides and peeking his head around the corner to check on the fallen officer again. "I think we need to get inside this building, we need to grab Stuart and get into this building to regroup. Look on the other side of the building for a door."

Fred first looks hesitant about moving. His back has been firmly planted against the wall since the two men dove for safety. He slides his feet along the wall until he is able to stick his head out far enough to check the side of the building for a door. A look back at Mitch and a nod of the head confirms that the only way into the building is on that side.

Even though Fred is much bigger than himself, Mitch knows that he is going to have to be the one that runs out to grab Stuart and carry him into the building. There is zero cover in the area between the building and where the fallen officer is and if Fred were to freeze up, he would surely get shot. A wave of the hand brings Fred back to Mitch where the younger man gives orders like a seasoned pro.

"You are going to have to use your rifle to get into that room. I don't care how many shots it takes, just blow that lock off. Once I hear the first shot I am going to go get Stu. I need you to help me once I reach the side of the building and close the door again once we are safely inside. Can you handle that?"

It is unlike Fred to be at a loss for words but after hearing the plan that Mitch came up with, his only response is an affirmative nod of the head. He slowly retreats to the opposite corner of the building and prepares his weapon to blast the hanging padlock. The few seconds it takes him to shoot off the lock is the most dangerous part of the plan. Fred will leave his body exposed to the shooter, even if it will only be for a brief time.

Mitch waits for the officer to ready his rifle, the fact that the shot sounded like it came from the west means that Fred will more than likely be hidden by trees to the shooter. When his friend disappears around the corner, Mitch begins to feel the adrenaline run through his body. During his high school football days, he learned how to use this rush of energy in a positive way. In this most serious of situations and seconds before he puts his life at risk to save his friend, Mitch finds the irony in the situation. In high school, when the game was on the line and he was given the ball, scoring a touchdown felt like a life or death situation. He is snapped back to reality with the loud pop of the rifle shot. Like a sprinter, he takes off at the sound of the gun.

Kevin M. Moehring

Chapter 16

His sprint to save his fellow officer only took a few seconds, but in that time, Stuart was able to raise himself up at the waist and look back at Mitch. The three loud shots from behind him were probably what woke him up and caused him to turn around. The fact that he was conscious made it much easier to move him to the safety of the ice cream building. As soon as Mitch reaches his side, Stuart throws his arm over his shoulder and forces his body to a standing position. The two men move quickly, as quickly as the can with Stuart hopping along with a bloody leg.

Fred is waiting for them at the open door to the building, helps bring Stuart inside and slams the door shut behind them. The three men are now all together for the first time since they left the Ferris Wheel a couple of hours earlier. They have each had their own strange experiences in the park, but this is the first time they will be able to put all the information together. Hopefully the collection of data will allow them to come to a conclusion as to what is indeed happening.

Stuart tries to sit himself down on top of some large cardboard boxes, but his weight is too much. The box rips open on the sides and drops the injured officer down on top of it. Blood has covered the entire lower part of his left leg. His face is pale, but his cheeks are red, more as a result of actually having to exert some energy, which Stuart hates to do.

Mitch makes his way to the injured man, pulls out his pocket knife and slices a hole in the pant leg. It is obvious that the shot went completely through his leg and exited the other side. The wound is halfway between the hip and the knee, with matching holes on both sides. Mitch stands up, looks around the room, and decides to take off his belt and wrap the strap of leather around the upper thigh to act as a tourniquet. Now that he has done the best that he can with the wound on Stuarts leg, Mitch turns his attention to the room they are in.

There doesn't seem to be much left in here except for a few boxes and a couple of wooden chairs. The windows where the customers are served is still intact but all that can be seen is the opposite side is the sheet of plywood. Fred has taken a seat in one of the chairs, next to the door. His head is hung low as if he is inspecting something on the ground between his feet. Stuart remains propped up on the opposite side of the room, holding his hands on the outside of his thighs. Mitch grabs the remaining chair and sits against the wall opposite the serving window, between the two men.

"Look, there is obviously something going on here. It's not every day you find a headless body chained to the front seat of a roller coaster." Mitch was ready to go on but was interrupted.

"Wait...you found what?" Stuart has no idea about what the other two officers discovered in their area of the park. He was trapped inside the tiny room of the carousel and had no way to reach them. "So there really are people out here hunting us?"

"Hunting us? I wouldn't say that. The only thing we know for sure is what we have found on a few pieces of paper. Fred and I both found basically the same list of names and resumes. I'm assuming that this is some sort of roster for the so-called players of whatever game is going on. Our names and faces are not on that roster, so I wouldn't say anyone is out here hunting us."

"But you didn't see what I saw. That's what I was trying to get you to come over and see on the ride." his voice tapers off at the end as he uses all of his energy to lower his leg into a much more comfortable position. "Once I turned the ride off and caught my breath, I went back to the room where the ropes were tied. They had been cut near the door and as I bent down to pick one up, something else caught my eye. I shined my flashlight onto the mirror, but I didn't see it. All I saw was my own reflection. Once I moved my flashlight away, the mirror lit up with a long message."

For the first time since they entered this room, Fred now raises his head. If he is going to be the hero and save the day, which would also bring the attention that he desperately seeks, then he would have to have all of the facts. "Well according to the list of rules, all the players started out on the carousel, that probably explains the ropes. What did the message say," he chimes in.

"At the top in large letters it said *CREW*, as if it has to make it clear who the message was intended for. I tried to memorize the rest of it but when people start shooting at me I tend to lose my focus."

"I think I saw the word *CREW* on one of the pages you grabbed off the door to the hut, Fred." Mitch makes a waving motion of his hand indicating to the other officer that he needs to produce the evidence he found. "I think it was on the map, come to think of it, I think I saw it on the back of my page, in the directions for the game."

The two men take out their sheets of paper and again arrange them on the ground in the middle of the ice cream shack. Mitch gets down from the chair and kneels beside them, so he can see every word that is written. He points to a line on the page of directions and again at several spots on the map. "Here, it says *CREW HQ* is off limits to all players. According to the map, this building here next to the Ferris Wheel is the *CREW HQ*. Does anyone know what this building is?"

Stuart is grunting as he tries to angle his head higher to get a look at the map. Fred is shaking his head as form of response before beginning to speak. "I don't think it's a public building, at least not one that I can remember. It looks like the place where the restrooms are located. It might refer to the offices where the owners and managers stay during the day."

"That's it! It's right there between the Ferris Wheel and main gate. From the outside it just looks like a pole barn but once you're inside you would think you were in an office building. I went there once with my father...I mean the sheriff, when there was a robbery a few years back. Now that we know that the people playing the game call themselves the *CREW* and we know where the headquarters is, we know where we need to go next."

Stuart makes a coughing sound, not the kind of sound that comes from choking on blood or anything. He makes the coughing sound to get the attention of the other two men. Once they turn their attention back to him with puzzled stares, he begins to tell the what the rest of the message on the mirror said. "First of all, with my leg like this, I doubt I will be getting anywhere near the Ferris Wheel or main gate. Secondly, if you would let me finish, the rest of the message said that there were three new players in the game. I don't really remember how it was worded exactly, just that they were definitely talking about us. So, like I was saying, there are people out there that are hunting us."

Fred is now on the edge of his chair, listening intently and scratching his head in bewilderment at the same time. "The message said that there were three new players in the game. That could be anyone. There is no way to tell that they were implying we were to be hunted. That message could have been weeks old."

"No Fred, the last few lines of the message made certain that even someone as naive as myself would understand who the three new players were." Again, Stuart makes a facial expression to let both of the men know that he was agony over his injury. "It said something to the effect that our heads were worth seventy-five grand, I think. At the bottom in large letters, it said the new players were the *LAW*!"

Kevin M. Moehring

Chapter 17

Mitch is now up and pacing the room, well pacing it as best that he can considering it takes exactly two steps to get from one side to the other. The message that Stuart told them he saw on the mirror was definitely putting the three officers right in the middle of whatever deadly game was being played. Once Fred confirmed, according to the list of game rules, that all messages will be communicated via the carousel panels, it was obvious to everyone that they were indeed the new players.

"I think it's clear to all of us that we are in danger. We need to figure out what are next move is or some kind of strategy that will keep us all alive." The desperation in his voice is apparent even when he clears his throat and tries to sound much more confident. "According to the map, whoever is running this thing is held up near the main gate. Somehow we have to get to that building and stop this."

"I'm content to just hide out in this building," Stuart adds while still applying pressure to the gunshot wound to his thigh. "Eventually someone, probably the sheriff, will come out looking for us."

"We can't stay here, Stuart. You were the one that found the message. There's a price on our head." Mitch reaches down and grabs one of the pieces of paper that had been laid out on the floor. "These guys are coming for us and it won't be long until they find us. Have you had a look at these guys, they are trained killers."

"We can't just leave him in this room, nor is he in any shape to go running around the park," Fred explains. "Mitch, I want to end this thing as badly as you do but we are no match for these guys. The guys on that list have been training for years to hunt and kill, not to mention that there is six of them and we only have two healthy bodies."

"Correction, there are only five of them now. I think it's safe to say that the body I found on the front seat of the roller coaster belongs to one of these faces." Mitch holds the list of players high above his head and shakes it violently for emphasis.

"So, there's only five highly trained killers out there somewhere looking to get rich off of our heads. That makes me feel so much better." Fred's face is now turning bright red with frustration. "I don't know about you, but I didn't sign up to be a cop so I could run around Graham Park trying to avoid a group of mercenaries."

The two men are now almost face to face, as if they would come to throwing fists at any moment. Stuart has been listening to the disagreement from the other side of the room and looking over the papers that are laid out on the floor. His focus is mainly being pointed toward the map of Graham Park. "Mitch, what time was it when you saw the Ferris Wheel?"

The question surprises the two other officers and breaks the tension that had been building in the room. Mitch and Fred look over at Stuart at the same time, both men reluctant to take their eyes off of the other. "It was a little after nine I think, why?"

"And it was right around midnight when the carousel started up, with me on it. The map has corresponding times listed on it for every ride, like a time when each ride will turn on." Stuart has moved his body so that his upper body is resting on his left elbow, which is working hard to hold up the weight. He uses his right hand to point at the times listed on the map for both the Ferris Wheel and carousel. "What time is it now?"

"It's almost two," says Fred after looking at his phone. "When is the next time on the map?"

Stuart runs his finger across the map looking closely for the times listed near the names of the rides and attractions. "It looks like the next time on the map is two-thirty."

Mitch has now moved closer to Stuart and studies the map from over his shoulder. "Yeah, looks like the roller coaster has the nearest time. That's probably where we should head next, at least to get a look."

The redness returns to Fred's cheeks, "If the map shows that something in the game is happening at the roller coaster at that time, then we should be as far away as possible."

"Fred, we need to put an end to this. Following the map and the times might get us close enough to these guys so we can arrest them. It sure as hell beats sitting in here and waiting for them to come find us." Mitch has always been one of those people who likes to use his hands when he talks, especially in times like this when he is trying to convince someone to do it his way.

Fred takes a look at Stuart, who is still seated on the floor nursing his wounds. "You think you can move on that leg?"

The injured officer looks at both of the men standing over him. His eyes dart from one to the other before he sticks out his hands in hopes that the two men will help him get to his feet. They oblige him and after a loud groan he is able to stand on his one good leg. Now that he is up off the ground he can see further past the two men than he could while he was on the ground.

"Guys, I don't think we have much time to debate this any longer. There's smoke coming in from under the door!" He almost loses his balance when he removes his hand from the wall that he's been using to keep him up, and uses it to point to the stream of black smoke that's coming in from the space at the bottom of the door.

Mitch quickly makes his way to the door and places his hand against it. The heat from the fire has made the inside of the door hot to the touch. "This is a wooden building and it is definitely on fire. We need to get out of here, quickly!"

Fred races over to grab his rifle, looks back at Stuart before walking over to Mitch and leaning in to whisper in his ear. "If we walk out of here with him, we are pretty much dead. I say he's on his own. Hell, I say we all split up and take our chances on our own."

Mitch looks at him with a disgusted expression. The thought of leaving Stuart to fend for himself never even crossed his mind. The fact that his fellow officer thinks it's the best idea angers him. He heads over to Stuart, throws the injured man's arm over his own shoulder, and leads him to the doorway. "You can do what you want but I'm not going to leave him behind."

The small ice cream stand is now almost completely full of smoke. Mitch is having a tough time holding up Stuart as they make their way toward the door. The anger and adrenalin are the only things pushing him through the thick wall of smoke with the extra weight on his shoulders. He bumps into Fred near the door and uses his free hand to give him a solid forearm push that moves him back. A swift kick of the hot door swings it open, exposing the roaring blaze of flames that has been working its way around the outside of the structure. With the door open, it takes almost no time for the intense heat of the fire to spread to the inside of the room. There is no choice left but to make a run through the flames. Mitch lowers his head and uses his free arm to cover the face of Stuart. After a deep inhale and a strong nudge to the back of his colleague, the two men are heading straight into the inferno.

Kevin M. Moehring

Chapter 18

The two men move rapidly at first, but it isn't long until the lack of fresh air and the burden of Stuarts wounded leg slow them down. It was only twenty feet from the burning building to the wooded area that follows the concrete walkway. It never occurred to Mitch that the burning of the building was just a ploy to get the three officers out into the open and there could easily be multiple assassins on the outside waiting for them. The two men clumsily fall off of the path and into the shrubs and trees.

Stuart practically collapses against a tree trunk and gasps for air. The short run from the building and the amount of smoke he ingested inside the ice cream building would leave the healthiest of people breathless. The men are captivated by the soaring flames that have now engulfed the building where they once felt safe.

Mitch has gotten back to his feet and recovered much more quickly than Stuart.

Deputy Thompson is now walking between the trees and bushes, shining his flashlight in different areas but making sure to not shine it out onto the concrete path. He doesn't want to give out his location to any of the killers who could be looking for them. His anger toward Fred before he left the room is no longer as important as finding his fellow officer. He had to struggle so bad to get Stuart to safety that he didn't have time to turn and look to see if Fred was able to make it out.

He turns off his flashlight and sits down next to Stuart under the tree. Hopefully Fred made it out safely because now the ice cream building is nothing more than burning rafters. The wooded protection that had been mounted to protect the glass windows acted as kindling and helped the fire spread to the entire structure. As they watch the fire slowly die out due to fact that everything that was flammable has now been burned, Mitch notices that the place where they ended up is probably impossible to detect from the pathway. There are several trees and overgrown bushes between where they sit and where the building was.

"It's probably about time to get to the roller coaster," Stuart says in a painfully strained voice. "We should probably get going if we are going to have any chance of making it on time.

"We have no chance of making it on time. Did you happen to see if Fred made it out of the building?" Mitch knows that it would have been nearly impossible for Stuart to see if their partner made it out, due to the fact that he kept forcing his head down in an attempt to keep the fire from burning his face. He asks the question anyway to make sure that Stuart is aware of the fact that they very well could have lost a friend.

"I didn't see him. You kept pushing my head down into my chest. You could just leave me here and go check out the roller coaster if you want." Stuart knows that Mitch would never leave him alone, especially if there was any chance the killers could be in this area.

"That's not going to happen. I just wish we knew what time was next on the map. We lost all of our evidence in the fire." The fact that all the papers were lost is not really important now but if there was ever going to be a trial, the evidence would be needed.

"Let me check the map and see when the next time is." Stuart reaches into his coat pocket and produces a stack of papers and begins to unfold the map. "While you two were whispering to each other, I grabbed all of the papers."

"I could kiss you right now!" Mitch scoots over so the two men could look at the map at the same time. "Looks like the pirate ship says three-thirty. That's the next time slot. That ride isn't too far from here, just down past the exit to the roller coaster."

Stuart is holding the map in both of his hands while Mitch is using the flashlight for visibility. Mitch is using his index finger to trace the path from where they are to where the pirate ship ride is. As his finger makes the last turn before getting to the ride, the map begins to shake badly. Before he can ask Stuart why the map is shaking, the far side of the map falls to the ground. He looks to Stuart who is now pointing back and the burning coals that was once the ice cream building.

Through the overgrowth Mitch can make out a dark figure moving toward the fire. He reaches for his rifle and tries to use the scope, so he can get a closer look. The man is large, carries a giant canvas bag and what looks to be a machete. He follows the figure as he circles the burning remnants of the building. The man is using the machete to poke at the coals and turn over large pieces of smoldering wood. Mitch slows his breathing, places his finger over the trigger to his rifle and prepares to fire.

Other than deer, he has never shot anything in his life. In the last thirty years, no member of the Twisted Timbers police force has ever fired a weapon while on-duty. He is now aiming down his scope at a dark figure who is only a few feet away from them. He allows his finger to rest on the trigger before applying the pressure needed to fire the round. The shot echoes through the silence of the night as does the sound of the body hitting the concrete.

Kevin M. Moehring

Chapter 19

Mitch had always been a good shot with his rifle. His father taught him at a very young age how to adjust for distance and wind speed when aiming at a deer far in the distance. The man he just shot was less than fifteen yards away and even at night, the shot would not have been considered difficult. He was able to see the reaction of the body as the bullet entered his neck, just below the jaw line. The knees buckled almost immediately and more than likely the man felt the burn of the bullet ripping through his flesh before he heard the sound of the shot.

"I didn't think you were actually going to shoot him!" Stuart sounds almost giddy with excitement at the result of the shot. "I almost wet myself when I heard the shot."

"I had to shoot him, he was looking around the burning remains of the building and for all we know Fred is still in there. I didn't want him to be able to collect any money from the body of our friend." Mitch secures his rifle and pulls out his flashlight once again. The fire has subsided to the point that it is emitting very little light now. "We need to go up there and look around. Can you walk?"

"I don't think so but I'm willing to try." The injured man struggles to reach his feet, using the sturdiness of the tree trunk he has been leaning against to support most of his weight. He takes two hobbled steps toward Mitch and gives him the thumbs up sign. "I won't be able to move quick, but I think I can make it. Honestly, I'd rather be anywhere else than here right now, so let's get going"

Mitch leads the way through the trees and shrubs, using his flashlight to point out any fallen branches that could be trouble for Stuart to get over. Once on the concrete path they pick up their pace slightly, still aware that there could be as many as four more killers somewhere in Graham Park. Mitch heads directly for the man that he shot and rolls over the body so that he can see his face. Just as he saw through his rifle scope, there is a large hole in the right side of the man's neck. He pulls out the list of the faces and names that Stuart was able to save before the fire started and quickly matches the dead man to the name of Vladimir Strotsky, a former KGB agent. Mitch pulls out the pen from his chest pocket, crosses off the name and face and returns the pen.

"Mitch bring me that list of names." Stuart is a few feet away and has opened the large bag that the Russian was carrying before being shot. The bag is open wide with the two cloth panels falling to the side, exposing everything on the inside. "There's a head in this bag!"

Mitch races over to where Stuart is seated next to the bag. There is indeed a head in the bag, covered with blood and looking up at him with mouth open. The lack of blood has turned the skin a pale shade of blue. Again, Mitch compares the face to the list of names, finds the corresponding face and crosses out the name of Roger Sheffield, a former member of the British Secret Intelligence Service. Apparently, Mr. Sheffield was once the private body guard to the Queen.

"That leaves us with only four more. Our odds are getting better." Stuart is speaking to Mitch while walking to the other side of the man that his partner just killed. He takes the machete out of the hand of the dead man and uses it to sift through the burning ruble. "There's no sign that Fred was inside here, but even if he was, I doubt there would much left of him to find. Should we get going to the pirate ship?"

Mitch is surprised by the sudden bravery of his injured friend. "Yeah, let's get going. According to the map, if we head up through these trees, we should come out in a perfect spot to see the ride."

The storm has finally moved in as the skies open up in a downpour just as the two men make it to the safety of the wooded area. The travel is slow due to the number of fallen branches, no doubt as a result of the harsh winter. Stuart has surprisingly taken the lead and is wielding the machete like a surgeon, clearing any brush that would cause trouble for him to cross with his bloody leg.

Mitch is happy to follow in the rear. The footing is far worse for him than it is for Stuart. Once the terrain has been matted down with footsteps and mixes with the rain that drips down from the branches, the ground becomes extremely slick. As they reach the top of a small hill, the area begins to get brighter. he checks his phone and sees that they are a few minutes late. Mitch races ahead to make sure that Stuart doesn't rush out into the open with his new-found bravado. He grabs him by the shoulder to turn him around and halt his impressive march to the ride.

Both men take a knee and use the scopes on their rifle to look at the pirate ship ride. *The Galleon* has been a favorite of the teenagers who visited Graham Park, with most riding it just after they get off the roller coaster. The large ship consists of eight rows of bench seats, with four rows on each side facing the middle. It works basically as a pendulum, being elevated by long poles that are brightly lit with purple lights. Once the riders have all been seated and secured behind their seat belts, an operator would throw a switch which would begin the ship on its swinging path. Once the ride was fully in motion the ship would swing from side to side, high into the air, with the riders screaming in excitement every time their side rose above the trees.

The two men are posted on top of the hill, with their rifles scanning the area around the ride. If you were to see them from a distance, you would think they were hunters who were taking aim at a large buck. Instead, the two men are searching for any sign of trained killers who are out here to end the life of anyone they find. The ride is lit up brightly, meaning that the area around it is aglow with the stream of purple lights that are mounted on the entirety of the large poles which swing the ship from side to side. *The Galleon* doesn't look nearly as intimidating now as it normally does when the riders are screaming at the top of their lungs.

The rain is nothing more than a drizzle now and the low growls of thunder are now to the east of Graham Park. With the ship moving quickly from side to side, it is difficult to follow through the rifle scope. It takes several passes from left to right before Mitch is convinced that the ship is indeed empty. He begins to search the area where the riders would wait in line to board the ship when he feels a strong whack on his back. It knocks him flying to his chest where his rifle lands a few feet in front of him. He rolls over quickly enough to see a mountain of a man beginning to swing a giant piece of wood at his face. He throws his forearms up just in time to absorb the impact and shatter the branch that the giant man had been swinging at his face.

The attacker is dark skinned and has large tattoos all over his arms. The ink seems to dance across his skin with every flex of his large muscles. He reaches down and places his large right hand onto Mitch's neck and uses his enormous body to add pressure, trying to suffocate the deputy. Mitch is struggling to breath, using both of his arms to try to remove the huge paw from his neck. No matter how hard he tries, he is unable to move the massive hand a single inch, not even long enough to allow himself a small gasp of air. He is seconds from passing out when the man's hand goes limp and his body falls to the ground next to him. From where Mitch is laying on the wet ground, Stuart looks like a warrior from ancient Rome with his blood covered machete held tightly in his left hand.

Kevin M. Moehring

Chapter 20

Stuart stands motionless for a few seconds. His hands are shaking, and it isn't long before he drops the machete. The shock of actually killing a person may be too much for him to handle. The look in his eyes lets Mitch know that his fellow officer has checked out mentally, very similar to how he looked in the moments after he was shot near the carousel. Things have gotten very serious for Stuart Johnson and judging by the sound of his breath, he is having a tough time adjusting. He has made tremendous efforts in the past to avoid violence and conflict at all costs. Now he stands over the body of a killer that he just put a machete through.

Mitch rubs his neck a few times before rising to his feet and brushing the mud and dirt from his uniform. He is shocked that such a large man would have been able to sneak up on them, especially through all of the broken sticks and branches that they had to navigate through. He walks over to Stuart and slaps him on the shoulder. "Thanks! You saved my life and you did what you had to do. When we get out of this mess, the first drinks at the Bottom Dollar are on me." Stuart looks at him and gives him a small grin, meaning he is alright with what he had to do. His stare is still a little glazed over but he appears to be coming out of the shock of killing another human being.

Mitch reaches into his shirt pocket and removes the list of names once more. When he was being choked, the man's face was only a few feet from his own, so he is able to find the corresponding name on the list with ease. He scratches off the name of Carlos Arroyo, a Colombian assassin who has an extensive resume of gruesome murders, mainly surrounding the cocaine industry. There are now just three names left on the list but there could be several more threats at the park if you count the people who are in charge of the game and are not listed on this roster. There is no telling how many men are hiding out at the headquarters building.

"The odds are getting better for us, but we need to make our way to the main building. The place that is labelled as headquarters on the map. We have to try and stop whoever is in charge of this whole thing. We also need to be aware that it is possible that they may have a small army in there." As Mitch finishes explaining to his fellow officer what he thinks is the best way to proceed, the pirate ship ride shuts down on its own. The lights fade to dark and the two men instantly reach for their weapons fearing that someone had to flip the switch manually. "I don't see anyone, the people in charge must have everything set on timers."

"Or they have them rigged to be able to control them remotely, like from the headquarters." The fact that aspects of the park could be operated remotely had never occurred to Mitch. Being thrust into such an intense situation has brought out every ounce of courage and police intuition that Stuart had been hiding for all of these years. "Let's start heading in that direction. Hopefully we can make it there without any more surprise attacks."

The two men tread lightly as they make their way down the small hill where they had been perched. They leave the body of the dead assassin laying under the trees where his body fell after he was stabbed through the chest with the machete. At first, they tried to move him, but his enormous stature required far more strength than either man could muster. Once they reach the concrete path, right next to the entrance to the pirate ship ride, they head north toward the front gate of Graham Park.

The giant Ferris Wheel looms in the distance showing the men which direction they need to head to reach the front gate. Even in the darkness, the large metal structure is still seen from almost any point in the park. They make their way past the carousel that once looked like it was going to explode in a cloud of smoke. They shine their flashlights from side to side as they reach the midway and the collection of buildings that host the carnival games and arcades. They separate for a brief period so that the can go on opposite sides of the Ferris Wheel before meeting each other at the other side.

The deputies make it to the building they were looking for without much trouble. Other than Stuart limping along and making moaning sounds at random times causing Mitch to fear they had been spotted and reach for his rifle, the trip was uneventful. The headquarters is in a building that most people who have visited the park would only notice if they needed a restroom. The long building is very normal looking with no features that would stand out. The lack of an eye-catching facade is a strong indicator that it does not contain anything that the paying public would be interested in seeing. This is also the only building in the park that is not painted in the same bright colors as the rest. Instead, the wooden shutters are painted brown to contrast against the tan color of the exterior paneling.

Mitch motions to Stuart that they need to work their way around the building and once again the two men take off in opposite directions. Mitch is the first one to find the entrance to the building. He waits patiently for Stuart to make his way around to where he is before going in. The building has no windows, so there is now way for the two men to know if it is occupied. Even though there is no way to tell how many men are on the inside, Mitch fears that his current run of luck doesn't bode well for them.

They check that their weapons are loaded and do their best to kick the door in and charge in like experienced police officers. Of course, they are anything but experienced and end up practically tripping over each other when the door opens far easier than they had expected. The one floor building is nothing but a long hallway, with a few doors scattered on either side. Both men are relieved to see the hallway is well lit, allowing them to return their lights to their pockets and carry their weapons properly with both hands. More importantly, they are relieved to see that the hallway is empty, both men expected to stumble in on a small platoon of gun toting soldiers.

Mitch takes the lead and slowly heads down the hallway. He stops near the first door and places his ear against it. He shakes his head to show Stuart that he didn't hear anything coming from inside the room. He slowly turns the handle and cracks the door open wide enough to get a peek inside. There is a brief moment of tension before realizing the room is empty. They file through the door and find a small room with nothing inside other than large stacks of computer equipment. Neither of the men know what the equipment is used for, but the nest of wires and multitude of blinking lights must mean the units are hard at work. Confident that there is nothing else in the room that will help them, they make their way back to the hall.

As they inch their way down the hallway, they can see a ray of light escaping below the door on the far side. Mitch walks right past the other two doors and heads straight for this door. Once again, he places his ear on the door and listens intently. He hears something, but he is unable to figure out what it is. He knows it's not voices but there is definitely activity on the other side of the door. He looks to Stuart and gives him a look that tells the other officer to be ready for anything.

The two men stand side by side, with rifles at the ready, as Mitch slowly opens the door. The room is extremely bright, and the rush of light takes a while for their eyes to adjust to. In this moment, they both hear a sound very familiar to them. Once you have heard the sound of a pump-action shotgun, you don't tend to forget it. The two men dive on either side of the door as the shot rips through the wooden door and the frame that surrounds it. The walls of the hallway trap the sound of the shot and it echoes throughout the space. Mitch sits up and looks through the bright light to see if Stuart is safe. He nudges himself close to the wall, trying to hide the best that he can. He failed to hear the pumping sound as the shooter reloaded but as he tries to stick his head around what remains of the door frame, the first thing he sees is the barrel of the weapon only inches from his face.

Kevin M. Moehring

Chapter 21

Mitch freezes for a brief second, fearful that any movement he makes will force the gunman to pull the trigger. His nose is so close to the barrel that he can smell the residue of gun powder that remains from the first shot. The bright light the room is emitting makes it impossible to see the person holding the gun on him but as his heart beats rapidly he figures it's a good sign that he is still breathing. If the person wanted him dead, chances are the back side of his head would be splattered all over the hallway by now.

"Get up son," comes the deep bellowing voice from behind the weapon. Mitch recognizes the voice instantly, not to mention the fact that nobody else has ever called him 'son'. "You too Stuart, get in here so we can take a look at that leg."

The two men rise to their feet and are beyond relieved to see that the person who fired the shot at them, and is now extending his hand to theirs, is Sheriff Thompson. The gray-haired man stands much larger than Mitch and is thicker in the shoulders. He has become sort of a legend in Twisted Timbers over the years for his ability to diffuse a situation using only his words. He has never seen the need to carry a weapon while on-duty, until now that is.

"Sheriff! Boy are we glad to see you." Stuart is heading straight for an office chair in the corner of the room. He is obviously relieved to take the weight off of his injured leg and to no longer have to be the most active member of the police force on scene. "What are you doing here?"

"Well Stuart, I knew something wasn't right when Mitch called me earlier and told me the Ferris Wheel was lit up. I made a few calls to the feds over in Portland, they'll be here in the morning by the way, and got in the truck and headed out here. You boys want to give me the rundown as to what has been going on." Sheriff Thompson looks at the two men as if he is waiting on them to give them a good excuse as to why there are dead men all over the park.

Mitch and his father pull up folding chairs near where Stuart is. The two younger officers give the sheriff a full description of everything that has happened so far, including the fact that they fear that Fred was killed in the fire at the ice cream shack. The sheriff sits quietly, listening intently and taking notes as the two men do their best to accurately describe the events that took place. There were several times when they talked over each other, mainly because they were having different experiences while they were separated in the park. The sheriff waves his hands while they talk to tell them which one of them should talk at a given time.

"OK boys, let me tell you what has happened on this end. About ten years ago, we got several calls that the Ferris Wheel was lit up well before the park was supposed to be open for the season. I decided to head out here to check things out for myself but when I got here everything was dark. I chalked it up to the kids in town trying to scare each other with more of those ghost stories they like to tell." The sheriff pauses in his story long enough to grab his thermos from the desk nearby and pour himself another cup of coffee. "I didn't think anything of it until a few weeks later when a groundskeeper here found a severed head hidden in the bushes. They were getting the park ready to open for the season and he found it laying off of the pathway over by the carousel. I talked to Mr. Graham about it, but he claimed to have no knowledge. We were unable to identify the head and sent it off to the Portland unit for further testing. That was the last I heard about it. I never really gave it a second thought until you called me last night."

"Dad...I mean Sheriff, do you think what they found back then is somehow related to what is going on now? I mean it seems a little farfetched to think that something like this could have been going on for ten years without us ever knowing." The dryness of his throat makes his voice much deeper than normal. He eyes his father's thermos of coffee but doesn't dare to ask for a cup. He learned that lesson very early in life when his father gave him a strong whack with a spoon when Mitch tried to take the last cup out of the pot one morning.

"I wasn't sure the two were connected, and I'm still not sure, but when I wasn't able to reach you, I thought I should get out here. Did you happen to check all the rooms in this building before coming to this one?" He looks at the two men with a knowing eye and takes a long warm drink from his mug.

The two officers look at each other before answering. They know that the sheriff will not be happy that they didn't follow protocol and clear every room before heading straight to the one with the light shining through the bottom of the door. "No Sheriff," Stuart finally utters to break the awkward silence. "We checked the first room, the one with all of the computer equipment. When we left that room, we could see the lights coming from this one and we came straight here." The injured officer has turned a little pink in the cheeks, with the judgmental eyes of the sheriff piercing a hole right through him.

"You guys were not very quiet either. I knew you were coming from the minute you opened that outer door. The computer equipment you found is what they call servers. If you would have taken the time to check the other two rooms, you would see that they are used to power all the things in those rooms. The other two rooms are connected, they tore down the wall between them, making one very large room."

"They? Who is they?" Mitch is eager to find out who is responsible for everything that has been going on, but his father sits calmly in the wooden chair and takes a slow drink of his coffee. How can his old man be so calm in a time like this, he wonders to himself?

"I'll get to that. That double room is filled with dozens of computer monitors and about ten television screens. They have the whole park wired with cameras and it looks to me like they are running some kind of game show on the internet. My guess is they are charging the viewers to watch the players take each other out, one by one." As he places his cup back on the counter, he points to the small closet on the other side of the room. "Mitch, go over there and wheel out my new friend."

Mitch is confused at first but rises to his feet and heads toward the small closet door in the opposite corner. When Sheriff Thompson says something, people usually listen and do what he says, another lesson Mitch learned very early in life. As he gets closer to the closet door he can hear muddled groans coming from inside. He opens the door with a quick swing and just like the sheriff inferred, there is a man sitting in an office chair, who looks up at him with large eyes. The man is no doubt thinking that he is being rescued. His eyes dart to the badge on the officer's chest and his head instantly hangs in shame once more.

Mitch grabs the back of the chair and wheels it out into the center of the room. Sheriff Thompson has succeeded in securing him with the use of duct tape and thick rope. The man looks far too young to be the mastermind of anything as lethal as the game that is going on, especially if it is linked to a similar event that happened a decade ago. Mitch notices the large red spot on the man's forehead, which is no doubt the result of the famous right hook the sheriff uses when things get serious.

"Take the tape off of his mouth so we can finish asking him questions. I was in the middle of my interrogation when you dummies decided to interrupt." The sheriff throws his feet up on the counter, once again looking cool and collected, as if he has not a worry in the world about how this whole mess will turn out.

Mitch on the other hand is sweating profusely and his heart still has not returned to its normal rate. He rips the tape from the guys mouth and the man lets out a loud scream. Mitch gives him a swift smack on the head with the back of his hand and tells him to be quiet. Violence had never been a forte of his but after the events of the evening so far, it has become increasingly more relevant. "How much have you gotten out of him so far?"

"Not much. He thinks he's a tough guy and hasn't said a single word. I was just about to practice some of the things I learned in the war in an effort to convince him that talking to me would be beneficial." Sheriff Thompson is slow to rise to his feet but once he does he towers over the younger man in the chair. Bill Thompson has always been able to get what he wants in life, usually without having to ask for it. Mitch likes the added effect the sheriff achieves by mentioning things he learned in the war, even though his father never served.

Now all three officers are standing in a circle around the man in the office chair. The prisoner's eyes dart back and forth as he tries to figure out which one of them is the most immediate danger to his well-being. He studies Stuart for a long time, the blood running down his leg is enough to convince anyone that he is a threat. The man twists his head in order to look at Mitch who stands firmly behind him. Mitch is possibly the most unassuming member of the trio, especially since the man can only see his head. Finally, the man returns his attention to the sheriff. He has already felt the power of the right hand, so it is obvious that the sheriff is not fooling around.

"I'm going to ask you some questions and I want answers. If you decide to stay quiet, my deputies and I will take turns beating the crap out of you until you beg us to stop. The choice is yours." The sheriff leans into the man's face to stress the importance of the words he is telling him. The man decides the only thing to do is to avoid eye contact and lowers his head to look at the linoleum floor. The sheriff brings his arm back and delivers a strong right hand to the man's cheek.

In a thud, the fist makes contact with the soft flesh and Mitch is certain he saw at least one tooth leave his mouth and fly across the room. Mitch has been a witness to his father's power several times before but this time it seemed to have a bigger effect than normal. "I suggest you answer his questions, he's just getting warmed up,"

Kevin M. Moehring

Mitch tells the man as a small stream of blood begins to flow down his chin.

"What do you say we start with an easy one, shall we. What's your name?" Mitch and Stuart sit back down in their chairs and watch as Sheriff Thompson does what he does best, get the information he wants. The sheriff walks around the chair giving a hard slap to the back of the head of the prisoner, and again asks him for his name. The man remains silent for a long time until he sees the sheriff pull a long hunting knife out of his pocket.

"OK...OK. My name is Steven Graham. My uncle owns this park. Are you happy now?" The prisoner hangs his head in defeat after giving up his name. The Graham name has long been a fixture in Twisted Timbers and dates back to the years of the gold rush. It never crossed the minds of the police officers that the owner of the park had anything to do with what was going on.

"You're telling me that old man Graham allows you to do this here? I find that very hard to believe young man. Now come clean with me or else I'll clean your flesh right off of the bone." Sheriff Thompson makes a slicing motion with his blade, making sure that Mr. Graham has a good look at it.

"I'm telling the truth! You asked me my name and I told you. I never said my uncle knew anything about what I was doing. My uncle and father haven't had a very good relationship of the past twenty years." Steven Graham is careful not to give out too much information, only telling the sheriff exactly what he asks.

"Mitch, get Mr. Graham on the phone. I think he should know what we found out. Tell him the F.B.I. will be here in the morning to sort everything out, it's best if he stays away until then." Mitch gets up from his chair as his father requested but stops once the meaning of what his father has asked sinks in. As if he knew what his son was thinking the sheriff continues, "there's a land line phone in the next room over."

Mitch exits the room quickly and the sheriff returns his focus to the man tied to the chair. Stuart follows Mitch with his eyes until he is out of sight before turning his head back to watch the sheriff. Anyone who has ever seen the sheriff in action knows that it is a spectacle to watch. The injured officer is confused as to where he should be or what he should be doing, so he just sits in the chair and remains quiet.

Sheriff Thompson kneels down in front of Steven, with the sharp knife blade aimed directly at the man's throat. "I'm going to give you the facts as we know them and any time I miss something, or you have something to add, I want to hear it. Do we understand each other?"

The captured man says nothing but even Stuart can tell that the man is defeated. He is unable to move and there is little chance that he would be able to escape his current situation even if he could. Steven Graham looks up at Sheriff Thompson and simply nods his head.

"Let's see, somehow you managed to bring six very deadly individuals to our quiet town, and stick them all inside our favorite amusement park. For some reason, every ride in the park remotely starts up at random times and lights up the night sky."

"The Ferris Wheel was used as the starting and ending time for the game. All the players knew this. As for the other rides, if you are able to kill another player with the ride somehow, you are given a fifty-thousand-dollar bonus. The people who are paying big bucks to watch this thing go crazy when someone is killed like that." The captured young man adds this little bit of information as if he is proud of the rules he has set up for the players to abide by.

"Well that clears up why the rides would randomly turn on. You're able to start them from your little control center next door?" The sheriff waves a hand toward the rest of the rooms in the building but since he wasn't expecting it, the hand wave makes Stuart jump.

"I can do just about anything from that room. I have access to anything in the park that is hooked to the power grid. It took several months for me to get things set up, just for you guys to come in here and ruin it before the game was over." After he says the last word, the man spits out a long stream of blood from his mouth that lands on the floor not far from the boot of the sheriff.

The sheriff responds with a slight chuckle before addressing the man again, "I'm sorry to crash your party but maybe my deputies are a little better than you gave them credit for."

"I wouldn't say that. I think they've been extremely lucky." Once again, the man has an oddly cocky attitude for someone who finds himself in a situation as dire as this one.

"I don't care what you think they've been, so far they've been able to hold their own against your team of trained killers." Sheriff Thompson gives a wink to Stuart, knowing the deputy isn't fond of violence and the fact that he stabbed someone to death will weigh on his mind far after this ordeal is over. "Let's get back to the facts. One of your killers somehow used the *Wood Splitter* coaster to take off another guy's head. Then my guys took out two of your other guys, one of whom had a head in his bag. Apparently, if I read these rules correctly, the killers are paid extra money if they bring back body parts as evidence of the killing. On top of all of that, you are in these rooms acting as the leader of the game and running all of the cameras that you set up. People are paying you money for the ability to watch everything go down. Am I right so far?"

"That's the big picture. You've missed a few details, like the giant increase in revenue I gained in the moments after the roller coaster killing. Not only are people watching the action that I am streaming online, I also set up a site that allows them to bet on the person they think is going to be the last man standing. So far we have about nine million dollars wagered since the time we started." The man seems impressed with the large amount of money he has generated. He looks at the sheriff with a smug grin and half a smile.

"Sheriff, can I interrupt for a second?" This is the first time that Stuart has said anything for quite a while and his voice rips apart the tension that had been building between the prisoner and the sheriff.

"Sure, go right ahead. The more we get out of him, the more we'll know." For the first time since the interrogation began, Sheriff Thompson returns to his seat and just stares at the prisoner.

"When I was on the carousel, someone fired a shot in my direction. It missed but caused me to take cover. Once the ride started up, I was able to get out of the little room. I saw Mitch and Fred coming to save me but before I reached them I was shot. What I'm wondering is why were there several ropes tied to some of the animals on the ride?"

Another small chuckle from the prison, "All of the participants in the game were tied to the carousel by yours truly. I worked very hard on tying the knots the best I could but I'm afraid they were tied tight enough. If they were unable to get out of the ropes then the ride would start up and pretty much slice their body in two.

Unfortunately, they all made it out long before the ride started up."

Stuart musters up the energy to rise his body out of the chair he has been sitting in. The blood has quit flowing from his leg, but the soreness and pain has intensified with the lack of adrenaline rushing through his body. "That doesn't make much sense to me, but if you say so. If all of these guys are the best killers on earth, why am I still alive? Whoever was shooting at me had multiple chances to take me out and he missed, twice."

Following these questions Steven Graham breaks into full-fledged laughter that comes from deep in his gut. "I think I know who was shooting at you and if he wanted you dead, you'd be dead. He has one flaw that the other killers don't. He is a former Ranger, the best sniper the Army has produced in decades. He is solely responsible for clearing a whole village in Afghanistan. What makes him different from the others is his conscience. His name is Jesse Meyer and he has a long family history of fighting for this country, he practically bleeds red, white and blue."

"So, you're saying he didn't kill me because I am American? If that's the case, then the odds are suddenly looking better for us." Stuart suddenly feels a strong surge of pain in his leg and falls into his chair again. "There's now three of us and only two of these crazies are trying to take us out."

"I'm not saying he won't kill you because you're an American, I'm saying he will only kill an American who deserves it. Once provoked, he is just as ruthless as any of these other maniacs. I wouldn't necessarily consider him an ally"

"By the way, we found your hat by the Ferris Wheel. I assume it's yours because we originally thought it belonged to a child, but I guess it could also fit a small man like you." Stuart looks down on the man with the disgust that comes from looking at the person who is responsible for the gunshot wound in your leg.

Sheriff Thompson sees that Stuart needs a minute to catch his breath and rises to his feet again. He is about to begin asking more questions of the prisoner, since he now seems more forthcoming with answers, so he can brag about the game that he has built. Before he can ask any more questions Mitch charges into the room with a red face and out of breath.

"Dad...Sheriff. You guys have to come here and see this." Mitch has his hand over his chest as if he needed to hold his heart to prevent it from beating out of his skin. "I think I found Fred. If it's him then he is still alive, at least he is for now. We have to hurry, or he won't be for too much longer."

Chapter 22

Sheriff Thompson instructs Stuart to stay put and keep an eye on their prisoner. He is happy to oblige because sitting in the chair is a lot less than painful than moving. The sheriff gives him directions about shooting at the first sign that the prisoner is trying to escape and turns to follow Mitch out into the hallway. They walk into the room directly next to where the interrogation was taking place. The room is filled with television screens, each one showing a different ride or attraction of Graham Park.

The two men stand silently in front of the screens for a long time. The sheriff eyes each of them intently, shifting his eyes from screen to screen before settling on one on the bottom row, directly in the middle of array. "I see it Mitch but tell me what I'm looking at."

Mitch leans closer to the screen so that he can point at certain aspects for emphasis. "This is the back side of the Ferris Wheel. I'm pretty sure that's Fred who is laying on the ground. It looks like there is a rope or chain around his neck." The figure on the screen is tiny and the quality of the video isn't the best, making it hard for the sheriff to see what his son is trying to point out.

Sheriff Thompson pulls out his glasses from his shirt pocket. He hates wearing his glasses, but his elevated age has started to take a toll on more than just his hips and knees. He knows that this is no time to miss details because of blurry vision. "Are you sure that's Fred? I thought you guys said he was killed in the fire at the ice cream building."

"We thought he was killed in the fire because when we stopped to look for him, he was nowhere to be found. We just assumed that he failed to make it out safely." Mitch is still out of breath and his words come out in an obvious sign that he is beginning to panic.

"Mitch, how many times have I told you boys about being thorough in your investigations. We can't just go around saying someone, especially a fellow officer, is dead. Without a body or any kind of evidence at all, we say that he is missing." He has harped on this point several times over the years. Even though the town doesn't have a high crime rate, he has always tried to keep his deputies informed and ready for any scenario.

"I get it but that is definitely Fred right there. If you look at the area where his left shoulder meets the ground, you can make out his badge, or at least I think that's what it is. The bigger problem is what your friend in there was telling us earlier. The game is over at sunrise and the Ferris Wheel will start up again to signal to the players that it's all over."

"And if the Ferris Wheel starts up, whoever that is out there will be left hanging by his neck!" It's not often that Mitch figures something out before his old man does, but when he does, Sheriff Thompson always finishes the thought. The older man thinks this gives his son the impression that he had it figured out at the same time. "It might be too dangerous to go out there and attempt a rescue but let's see if our newest friend can help us out at all."

The two men rush back to the room and find that Stuart has made his way back to his feet. He is standing over the man and seems completely out of breath. The prisoner now has a few more bruises on his face than he had when the two Thompson men left the room. "Stuart, you should be sitting down and resting. We need to get some more information out of this guy, so we need him to be able to move his mouth, otherwise I would let you continue."

Mitch can tell that his father is beyond upset at the way his deputy treated the prisoner, just by the tone of his voice. Stuart also realizes that the sheriff is not happy with his behavior and gives him an apologetic look before limping his way back to the chair. He once again sits quietly in the background as Sheriff Thompson addresses his prisoner.

"Tell me what time the Ferris Wheel is scheduled to turn on once again? What time is this whole charade supposed to end?"

The man twists his head as best he can, so he can look at the clock that is on the wall to his right. "Looks like you are running out of time. Sunrise is due in about twenty minutes and then the ride turns on and the game is over."

The sheriff looks at his watch and without giving the man the decency of a look, continues on with his questions. "You set this whole thing up and rigged all of the rides to turn on at certain times, so you should be able to turn them off."

"That's not how it works. The game program was written in a way that it cannot be changed or altered until the entire game has run its course. People are paying a ton of money to watch what goes on here, the last thing they want is to have someone change the rules right in the middle of the game. My father had an issue with the same things over the years, so we have learned to not let that happen again. Do you know how much dough I would lose if I didn't take that precaution? You don't get to be in charge of an event like this without having learned some lessons over the years."

"We need to shut down the Ferris Wheel before it turns on, the life of one of my deputies is at stake." This is the first time that Stuart has learned about the predicament that Fred is in and even though he doesn't know all of the details, the urgency in the voice of the sheriff lets him know the situation is serious. "There has to be a way to cut the power to the ride. Where is the electrical lines that you used to take over control of the rides?"

"They will do you no good either. As you well know, this area is a hotbed for power outages. Everything in the park has been hooked to multiple power sources to avoid any loss of signal during the event." Once again, the man looks over his shoulder at the clock. "Just fifteen more minutes before your friend becomes a human piñata!"

Mitch races off to the room where he was able to use the phone to call the park owner at his home. When he was there earlier he remembered seeing the group of radios with earpieces that the park security guys use. He grabs one and nestles the small speaker into his ear. He grabs another from the charger and races back to his father. He runs into the room and hands the other radio to Stuart, who looks at it oddly. "I'm going out there but Stuart you are by far the most computer savvy of the three of us. I need you to go over to that room and see if you can make heads and tails of the system. Maybe you will be able to watch my back without having to limp around."

"Sure Mitch, but what about this guy? We can't just leave him here unguarded. I'm sure he will try to escape." There has never been anything happen as long as he has been on the police force as extreme as what they are experiencing now, yet Stuart still finds a way to be far more level headed and think through all of the possibilities with ease.

"I'll just shove him back in the closet," chimes in the sheriff with his deep, masculine voice. "Mitch, we don't have a lot of time left, so we need to get moving. Help Stuart to the control room while I shove this guy in the closet. Grab a radio for me while you're in there."

"Wait. You're going out there with me?" The look he got from his father was all the answer he needed. Now Mitch isn't sure what he is worried about more, saving his friend and fellow deputy or keeping his father and sheriff of the town safe from the three remaining killers who are still on the loose.

"You're damn right I'm going with you. Nothing happens in this town without me being a part of it. That is why the good people of this town have given me the title of sheriff. There's no way I'm sending you out there without being by your side." With his final word he begins to wheel the prisoner back into the closet from which he came, and Mitch helps Stuart to his feet.

Kevin M. Moehring

Chapter 23

Mitch returns from the control room with a radio for his father and they both give a check of the system to make sure that everything is working properly. Once the men are confident the headsets are all functional, they quickly take off toward the Ferris Wheel. Once they leave the headquarters, they follow the concrete path that will lead them to the back side of the ride.

The tall metal structure stands higher than anything else in the area and acts as a beacon to anyone in the park. The men move quickly, Mitch leading the way due to his much younger legs, making sure to scan the areas they pass for any sign of one of the three killers lurking in the shadows. Periodically through the short trip, Sheriff Thompson will give nuggets of advice to his son. Make sure to only aim your weapon in the same place that your flashlight is shining or don't shoot at anything before you are sure what it is you are shooting at, both points that Mitch has heard his father advise him on numerous hunting trips growing up.

The younger Thompson reaches the ride a few steps ahead of his father, races over to where the man is still passed out at the boarding area. He pulls his phone out to check the time before yelling back to his father, "come on, we only have six minutes left."

The unconscious man lays motionless as the two men look him over. Sheriff Thompson grabs his wrist, so he can check for a pulse while Mitch focuses his attention on the thick chain that is wrapped around the man's neck. This is the moment that both men realize this is not Fred. Having studied the page full of killers involved in this game, Mitch is certain that this man is Jesse Meyer, the former soldier.

The other end of the chain is threaded through the thick metal beams that hold the canopies that cover the chairs of the ride. His body is propped up in a position that allows his upper body to lean against the back of the passenger car. The way his body has been positioned it looks like he is waiting to ride the wheel backwards, looking in the opposite direction of the rotation of the ride. "Stuart, can you give me the time?"

"You have about three minutes, are you able to get Fred out of there?" Stuart is speaking in a panic rush, his words all kind of mix together as if his hands are moving frantically trying to visually extract them from his lips.

"We're working on it but it's not Fred. It's the former Ranger that was shooting at you. Any sign of Fred at all or the other two killers?" Mitch has been tugging at the chain and padlock to try and find a weakness in the way it has been connected. So far, he has been unable to gain even an inch of slack. The weight of the man is acting like an anchor and pulling the chain too tight to allow Mitch to wiggle it at all.

"I haven't found them yet, but I am getting the hang of this computer system. It's far more advanced than anything we have at the station. Did you know there was a camera on us when we were interrogating the prisoner?"

Mitch lets his comments go without answering him. He is far too focused to worry about what the rest of the internet world heard a few minutes earlier. Even though the man who is attached to the back of the seat is not their friend, the two men remain focused on freeing him. It doesn't matter that this man had come to Graham Park with intentions of killing men for money or that he is probably the person who put a hole through the leg of Stuart.

"He has a pulse, more than likely he is just unconscious. Have you been able to figure out how to get him out of the chain?" Sheriff Thompson is now tugging at the large links of the chain around the chest of the fallen soldier.

"I don't think there is a way to get him out. I'm afraid we are going to have to watch him," before he can finish his last sentence, the lights along the metal poles that support the wheel begin to power on. Mitch frantically tugs at the chains a few more times but he is still unable to move the tight metal links. The Ferris Wheel is now fully lit and he can hear the gears begin to turn and start the long, slow rotation of the passenger cars.

For a lack of knowing of anything better to do, Mitch climbs into the seat that is on the opposite side of the killer's limp body. It is nothing more than a few flat pieces of steel that form a small bench type seat. He looks at his father who has begun to slap the face of the unconscious man trying to bring some life into him. Mitch plants his knees on the bench seat, lays his waist at the top of the back support and reaches behind the seat with both hands. He shoves his arms into the armpits of Jesse Meyer and bends at the elbow in an attempt to lift the man and stop the chain from cutting off his airflow.

The ride is in top speed now, which is still a crawl. It usually takes a full two minutes for a car to make the entire revolution. Sheriff Thompson looks on as his son is doing everything he can to hold the much larger man and prevent his hanging. Mitch is screaming, nothing important, just repeating the man's name in hopes that he will come to. About a quarter of the way around, his yells are matched by the much louder groans and the deep grunts from the fallen Ranger.

When he first opens his eyes, he begins to flail his arms about, almost causing Mitch to lose his grip. Luckily, the younger officer is in far better shape than the others and manages to hold the man tightly. When their gondola reaches the top and begins its descent, Jesse Meyer is able to locate the large bar that stops the seat from rocking out of control. He puts both of his feet on the bar and uses his thigh muscles to relieve some of the pressure on Mitch's biceps.

"Any idea how we are going to get out of here?" The tone of his voice is unlike anything Mitch has ever heard before. Until you have heard the words of a man who thought his life was over, you would not know what the sound was.

"I have no idea, but the Sheriff is here, and I have a guy in the control room keeping an eye on things. We're going to get you off of this thing." The calmness in the other man's voice has caused his heart rate to slow drastically.

"Hey guys, I have some good news and I have some bad news." Mitch hadn't expected to hear anything from Stuart and when he heard his voice it caused him to jump slightly. A slight groan from the soldier snapped him back into his current reality and Mitch regained his grip on the man's upper torso. "The good news is that Fred is most certainly alive. The bad news is that he is in the middle of the water park area and is having a fight with one of our friendly killers. Judging by some of the moves this guy has, I'm going to guess that it's the

Japanese guy. It doesn't look like Fred is going to be able to last much longer."

Out of the corner of his eye, Mitch notices his father take off in a sprint. He tries to use his radio but with both hands full at the moment, there is no way for him to tell his father that it isn't a good idea to go alone. Their gondola has now completed its first trip around and slowly passes through the loading area. The former Army Ranger uses the brief time he has with firm footing to readjust his shoulders and slightly loosen the chains. In the mere seconds where he was actually able to put his feet on solid ground, he has effectively removed most of his chest from the chains. He moved quickly and every time the chain tightened on his neck he would let out a soft moan.

What was once a tight chain that was cutting off the circulation, is now much looser. He is still unable to free himself completely, but can now turn and face Mitch. As the ride once again starts to raise them high above the ground, the man uses his own strength to hold his body in place. He hangs over the back of the canopy and faces Mitch but now that the eminent danger has subsided, the two men give each other a relieved look.

Once they reach the apex of the circle, the ride suddenly comes to a stop. From high above the other attractions at Graham Park, it doesn't take long to find his father. He looks like a small dot streaking across the pathway hundreds of feet below. When the ride began moving, Mitch tossed his rifle aside and did what he had to do in order to save the unconscious man. Now that he is stuck so high above the ground, he wishes he had it with him so he could use the scope to keep an eye on his father.

"Stuart, the sheriff went toward the water park. Keep an eye on him. The Ferris Wheel stopped, and we are stuck at the top." He loses sight of his father as he winds beneath the trees and makes his way toward the water park. Mitch turns and looks at Jesse Meyer and starts working on the chains again. They are now so twisted that it is hard to tell which strand of chain is actually still wrapped around his neck. In the back of his mind there is a small part of Mitch that thinks it might be wise to leave this trained killer confined in the very chains he is now working to free him of.

The two men continue to work to untangle the chains until finally Jesse Meyer is able to free his neck and climb over the back of the seat. Mitch helps him over and for a brief moment they find themselves in a very awkward embrace. The relief of getting his body free of the chains far outweighs the fact that they are stuck hundreds of feet in the air together, one a police officer and the other a trained killer for hire.

Mitch skips all of the normal introductions two men would make when they first met a new person. Instead, he opts to fill the man in on most of the details that he knows up until this point and how the man might as well stay put and turn himself in when the feds arrive shortly. There is a lengthy period of silence and the rescued man does not say a word in response to what Mitch tells him. They take turns looking over the side of the car, scanning the ground hundreds of feet below for any sign of life. The orange sun is beginning to rise high above the trees, giving the two men an unobstructed view of the Nehalem River and the rest of Graham Park.

"Mitch, you need to get down from there as quickly as possible. I couldn't see exactly what happened but Fred somehow managed to get the upper hand on the Japanese guy. He managed to hit the guy over the head with a rock or something. He hasn't moved in several minutes." The words cut through the calmness that the morning had brought to the situation and startle Mitch at first. His ride companion looks at him awkwardly, unable to hear what is being told to him through his earpiece. The change in the expression on Mitch's face makes it clear that something has happened. "I tried to follow Fred when he left the body, but I don't quite have the hang of this system yet. The next thing I was able to see was the body of the sheriff. He is laying on the ground in the middle of the midway."

"Stuart, get me off of this ride. Get me down from here now!"

"I have been trying to figure out how to do that since you got stuck. This computer system is far too complex for my brain. I don't know that I can do it." The voice coming over the radio is obviously stressed and strained. "I have called the Portland office several times to make sure they are sending a computer expert with them. They should be here in a couple of hours and we'll get you down then."

"A couple of hours! I can't wait a couple of hours. By then who knows what these killers will have done to my father." Mitch is screaming at the voice on the other end of the radio, even though he knows fully that it is not going to change things.

"Mitch, I get that. I have tried everything I can think of, but I can't hack into the system. I have even pulled the prisoner out and threatened him with more violence but he's not talking." The pain in the voice of Stuart is obvious, meaning things are definitely not looking good for the sheriff.

"I guess I have no other choice. I can't leave him down there all alone. He wouldn't leave any of us out there all by ourselves." Mitch is now speaking quickly and rushed. His eyes are jumping around looking at any and everything he can, trying to figure out a way off of this ride.

"What are you going to do?" Jesse can only hear half of the conversation but knows that Mitch is desperate to find a way to the ground.

"I'm getting down from here. You can stay but I have to get off of this thing. The feds will be here in a few hours and they will have someone smart enough to override the computer system and get you down. I think I can slide down this pole and work my way to the frame of the ride. From there I should be able to work my way all the way to the ground."

"That is probably not a wise decision. We're a few hundred feet in the air and you think you're going to climb out there without a safety rope? I get that you're trying to save the sheriff, but falling to your own death is not the right way to go about it." The man speaks to Mitch with a mind of reason, like a person who has known the deputy for many years.

"It's not just the sheriff who's laying on the ground, it's my father. I'm getting down there no matter what I have to do. He would do the same for me if I were in the same position."

Chapter 24

As he begins to stand up on the seat of the passenger car, Mitch is starting to regret his decision already. His hands are holding on to the cold steel tightly as he steals a look down. The sheer distance of the fall would surely be enough to kill him if he was unable to keep his grip. Slowly he lifts his right leg over the edge and struggles at first to find somewhere on the other side to put it down.

The frost from the cool night air has made everything a little more slippery than he expected and luckily his whole body isn't over the side of the seat before he loses his balance for the first time. He puts all of his weight on his right foot and lifts his left over the metal backrest of the seat. He tells himself repeatedly to not look down, that would add to the amount of fear he is feeling. He is now somewhat seated on the backside of the seat, not too different from how the soldier was perched when he was trying to save himself from being hung by the chain.

Standing outside of the safety of the seat makes the severity of the situation sink in more. The long metal pole that he is standing on runs all the way to the center of the ride. He judges the distance carefully and decides that the added moisture on the beam would make it impossible to walk across while standing. He begins to lower his body by bending slowly at the knees. He cautiously begins extending his hands, one at a time, until they are both on the pole out in front of him.

His plan is to move along the length of the pole while sitting on it, much like a kid would ride on a wooden horse. With his legs straddling the pole, it gives him much less of a chance of slipping off. Mitch turns to the soldier in the gondola and gives him a nod and a nervous look. That glance was more for his own confidence rather than assuring the other man that everything would be alright. His father is in need and he is going to help him.

One last call on the radio to tell Stuart that he wants to know of any changes to the sheriff's situation, and Mitch slides his hands out along the cold, wet metal.

He pulls the rest of his body forward in a clumsy motion. The wetness of the steel helps to slide him forward, but he only moves a few inches at a time. The trek is slow and physically demanding, his thighs are burning from the tight grip he keeps on the pole and his biceps and forearms have not worked this hard since high school.

He can feel the heat from the early morning sunshine that is hitting his face. Bit by bit he is making his way across the pole. It is taking him much longer than he would like but he has yet to have a feeling that he was in danger of falling. With every pull of his arms, the inner structure of the Ferris Wheel gets closer and Mitch has begun to plan his route down. The entire thing is made of steel poles and long chains. He hopes that there will be enough places to hold on to, so he won't have to take any dangerous chances.

Mitch is dripping with sweat as he reaches the inner part of the wheel. The long piece of steel that he has been moving along now meets a collection of diagonal metal beams. He was observant when he was making his way along the first beam, which now gives him the confidence that he knows which direction he needs to move. He grabs the first of the slanted beams, slowly transfers his body on top of it, and slides down the twenty feet to the end. Moments later he is back to his feet and slowly walking along another beam that will take him to the opposite side of the large center gear of the wheel.

The only thing that separates Mitch from the safety of the ground below is about forty feet of steel that he must travel down to reach the bottom gondola. Once again, he sits on the steel beam and straddles it as he did before. This pole is sharply slanted down meaning it takes far less energy to pull his weight forward. The trip is going smoothly when he first heard the sound of Stuart come through the earpiece.

"Mitch, you need to hurry. There's a large black man making his way toward the sheriff with a rather large knife in his hands." Hearing the sound of his voice actually had a calming effect on Mitch. He had been all alone for the last few minutes as he navigated his way down the Ferris Wheel and to know that he wasn't alone made him feel better.

Mitch moves much faster and once he reaches the point where his beam meets the bottom car, he leaps down to the seat and rolls to the ground below. It was less than athletic but he is back to his feet and running toward the midway without missing a beat. He waves up to Jesse Meyer to let him know that he made it safely and makes his way through the park. His mind considers for a moment if it was foolish to leave a murderer all alone, and able to make an escape, to rush to his father.

It doesn't take him long before he can see the man standing over his father's body. From where he is, the man looks like he could be a giant. He is shirtless, and the muscles of his abdomen are dark and tight. He holds a large sword over his head that causes the veins in his arms to look like they are going to pop right out of his skin. Mitch continues his mad dash, without a thought about what his move would be. He has no idea if the man has already used the sword on his father or is getting ready to begin his assault.

In a rush he approaches the man from behind. His feet are landing hard on the ground as he tries to be as fast as possible and is not worried about remaining silent. When he nears the man, he lowers his shoulder, as if he was making a tackle on a running back. The sound of his steps must have alerted the attacker and just as Mitch is about to hit him, he turns around. Mitch drives his shoulder into the man and both men tumble to the ground. It might not have been the safest thing to do but it had the desired effect. The man who was once standing over his father with a raised sword, is now laying on the ground next to him. For being such a big man, the man is far more agile than you would have thought. He is quicker to his feet than Mitch is and uses his quickness to grab the deputy by the neck. After the tackle, the man lost his grip on his sword, Mitch can see it a few feet away as he is being urged to his feet by the strength of the killer.

The man easily lifts him into the air, high above his own head. He is adding pressure to the neck, making it hard for Mitch to catch his breath. He has been through so much in the last few hours and now he is being choked out by a man who appears to be twice his own size. He hits the ground in a thud and it takes him a moment before he realizes what has happened. He heard the shot, of course, but it came from such a long distance that it wasn't loud enough to register over his fight for air.

When he fell from the grip of his attacker, he landed softly on top of the man's body. Mitch makes his way to his feet, rubs his neck for a bit and looks down at the remaining half of the large man's face. The shot has torn off most of the top side of the killer's head, almost from one ear to the other. It takes a long minute before Mitch remembers why he had rushed over to this area of the park. He slowly walks over to his father and does a quick scan of his body, before falling to his knees and screaming loudly into the early morning sky.

Kevin M. Moehring

Chapter 25

As tears roll down his face, Mitch looks down at the body of his father. The sheriff lays on his back on the cold concrete ground. His right hand is clutched at his chest, covering the badge that he was so proud to wear for many years. The pool of blood the fills his shirt and surrounds the area where his hand rests is the only sign of injury. Mitch reaches down and grabs his father's right hand and holds it in his own.

His skin is cool to the touch, obviously his father has been dead for a few minutes, meaning he was probably dead before the mercenary showed up with his sword. No matter how fast he would have been able to get over to this side of the park, it is unlikely he would have been able to change the results. Now that he can see the area of the wound, Mitch can see that his father died of a single, well place stab wound. Whatever weapon the killer used, pierced through the skin in the area around the heart and judging from the amount of blood, must have sliced through several arteries.

Since his mother passed away when he was a young boy, Mitch has relied on his father for everything. The one time that his father really needed him, he was too far away to be able to help him. His thoughts dart between childhood memories and how drastically his future is going to change without him around. He looked up to his father, much like many residents of Twisted Timbers did. Bill Thompson was always a calming force in the rare instances when things in town became hectic.

"Mitch, I'm sorry. I don't really know what to say to you in a time like this. I wish I could say something to make it better. I wish I was able to give you an official story as to what happened but like I said, I wasn't able to keep up with everything." Stuart speaks with a low mellow tone, obviously saddened by the death of his boss.

The simple words from his fellow officer cause Mitch to break down. He sobs uncontrollably and loud enough to be heard throughout Graham Park. The tears flow freely until he feels a comforting hand on his shoulder. He spins around quickly in fear and is confronted by the very man he saved from sure death moments earlier. He lacks the ability to muster enough energy to fight the man, drained from losing the one person who has been a constant in his life.

Mitch returns his father's hand to his chest and faces the man standing over him, with weapon in hand. "If you're going to kill me, go ahead and do it. I have no more energy to fight."

The man extends his arm and offers his hand to the beaten deputy. He then helps Mitch to his feet and allows him the time needed to gather himself. "If I wanted to kill you, you would already be dead. In fact, if I didn't save you from the crazy Kenyan, you would already be dead. My name is Jesse Meyers. I'm a former Army Ranger and a trained sniper but I'm nothing like these other guys. I'm not a crazy killer."

"Was that you who took him out?" Mitch had almost forgotten about being treated like a rag doll by the large black man. "How were you able to get down from the Ferris Wheel so quickly?"

"It looked like you needed some help. I guess all of those years in the Army kind of brain washed me. I hate seeing another American lose their life." The man has now lowered the large weapon and leans against it as he talks. Mitch hadn't noticed it while they were trapped together on the ride, but his face paint is now smeared and far less effective now that he is out in the open.

"Well I guess I owe you some gratitude. Unfortunately, I am still going to have to arrest you. The F.B.I. is on the way." Mitch hadn't really considered the fact that the soldier is only one here who is currently holding a weapon. That may make it a little more difficult to arrest him, but Mitch is hoping that his patriotism will persuade him to do the right thing.

With a bit of a grin on his face, the soldier turns and starts to walk away from Mitch. He is not running or jogging even, he just slowly walks away from the deputy. He is heading for the trees just next to the carnival games and stops before heading in. "I don't think you will be arresting me, you have far more things you should be worried about. The way I see it, you saved my life and I saved yours. Now it's even."

Mitch watches as the man disappears into the trees. He doesn't have the strength or energy to chase after him, so he returns to the ground next to his father. Once again, he grabs his right hand and holds it in his own. He uses his left hand to remove the badge from his father's chest. He rubs his fingers across the bronze star, soiled with the blood of his father, before placing it in his pants pocket. He kisses his father's forehead, stands up again, and begins the lonely walk back toward the front of the park. He has not yet felt the anxiety and fear that one usually feels when losing his father, but he is sure that he will be hit soon enough with a swarm of emotions.

Kevin M. Moehring

Chapter 26

The walk back to the front of the park feels much longer than it should. Mitch should be celebrating the success of the biggest case to ever hit Twisted Timbers. Instead, he is lamenting the fact that he was unable to save his father. Stuart has been talking to him in his ear for the entire walk, but he just keeps his silence and walks on. The flashing lights of the countless government vehicles that have ascended on Graham Park as a result of the evenings activities pierce through the wrought iron fence in front of him.

As he walks through the office building where he last left Stuart, he is forced to side step several guys in dark suits. When the feds show up to a crime scene, they come out in full force. Stuart is still seated in the control room, his back to the assortment of monitors and television screens. A large man who fits the stereotype perfectly is standing in front of him, asking questions and writing down the answers in his notepad. When Mitch walks into the room, everyone seems to go quiet and stop their investigation.

Mitch looks around the room, several guys are walking in and out of the room with laptops and long cables. Others are dusting for fingerprints and taking photos of every corner of the room. Without saying a word, Mitch turns around and returns to the room where he first found his father. The room is basically empty, meaning the guys from Portland must not know about their special guest in the closet.

Mitch rushes to the closet door, throws it open quickly and unloads on the man with a few well-placed punches to the face. The sound of the man screaming draws the attention of the agents in the area and they rush into the room and stop the melee. Mitch grabs the back of the chair, pushes the man to the hallway and into the control room. He shoves Steven Graham across the open floor until he comes to a stop near the feet of the large man who appears to be running the investigation.

"This is the man who is responsible for everything. His name is Steven Graham and his uncle is the owner of the park. My father interrogated him and apparently this isn't his first time putting on an event like this." Mitch walks across the room and takes a seat in an open chair next to his fellow officer. "I'm sure he will be more than willing to answer all of your questions."

"Thanks. My name is Special Agent Walker. Looks like you folks stumbled upon a pretty big bust up here. We have heard rumors of these things taking place in several places in the Northwest, but we have never had any evidence." The agent is writing furiously in his notebook, trying to record everything that has been told to him so far.

"We are pretty sure there was a similar event in this very park about ten years ago but the only person who would know anything about it is the sheriff...sorry, was the sheriff." He finds it hard to actually say the words, finding it easier to refer to the dead man as the sheriff instead of his father.

"That may be true. I'm sure we will get plenty of useful information once our computer guys get into the hard drives. They are the best at what they do. Excuse me while I go and check on their progress, the early indications are that this system is very advanced. They didn't say it would be impossible to hack, just that it may take more time than normal." As the man exits the room, Mitch has his eyes fixed on the man responsible for all of this madness.

"You guys think you won, don't you? Look at the big screen at the top." The man is still tied in the rope and nudges his head in the direction of the screens. "That is more money than a lot of small countries make in a year. I think all of your heroics were good for ratings, which means it is good for my wallet."

Mitch turns to look at the screen the man is talking about and notices the enormous number the man is referring to. "You think you are ever going to see any of that money? I doubt you will ever see the light of day again. You are responsible for the deaths of six men here, including a sheriff. I am going to see to it that you spend the rest of your miserable life in prison."

"You know what all of that money buys me? It buys me the best lawyers in the country. Hell, with that much money, it could even buy me a few judges." Given the current predicament, the man is far happier than he should be. "Besides, like I told you earlier, we have been doing this for a long time. My father started putting the *Crew* together when I was just a teenager. We know how to cover our tracks and we always plan for every contingency."

"What is that supposed to mean? I doubt you had planned for me to just happen to drive by last night and interrupt your little game. The only game you'll be playing in the future is hide and seek with a few sex starved inmates." Mitch gets up to walk out of the room and gives the man a final punch in the face before he exits. "Stuart, I'm going to check with Agent Walker and see how his guys are doing with getting into that system. Have you seen Fred wandering about?"

"I haven't seen him since he was able to beat the Japanese fellow. I thought he was heading in this direction but once the feds showed up, I haven't had much access to the camera feeds."

Kevin M. Moehring

Chapter 27

Mitch walks into the third room of the narrow office building, the one with the large computer servers and the rats nest of wires. Nothing in the room looks familiar to the young officer. There are several men in suits who are connecting and disconnecting wires in rapid fashion. The fact that anyone could have that much knowledge of how a computer system this intense operates, is mind boggling to Mitch. The only computer experience that he has is the few beginner's classes he took at the high school and the old system that the police station uses.

"Agent Walker, any word on how long it is going to be before your guys are going to be able to get into the system and give us a better idea as to what was going on here?" At first, he feels like he may have asked the question in his head, due to the lack of a response from the agent.

"They tell me it won't be that hard to get into the mainframe, but it is going to take some time to pull up the individual files and camera feeds. Probably going to be at least another hour or so. You've had a long night, why don't you go home and get some rest and give me a call when you feel up to answering some questions."

He had never even considered the fact that he is working on his second full day without any sleep. The minute Agent Walker mentions getting some sleep, Mitch lets out an uncontrollable yawn. "Yeah, that might be for the best. I'll give you a call later this afternoon." Mitch gives the men working on the servers a final glance before turning and exiting the room.

He makes his way down the hallway but decides to stop in and talk to Stuart one last time before leaving. "Stuart, I'm heading home to get some rest, you should do the same thing." He plops down in the chair across from Steven Graham. "There isn't much we can do here. They are working on getting into the system and it will be at least an hour before they know anything else. I'm kind of anxious to see how much they can find out from the videos so we can fill in a few of the blanks we have."

"I'm alright Mitch, besides, I'd rather stay and make sure they take care of the sheriff's body properly." He stops after mentioning the body, as if he just realized for the first time that he is not only talking about the sheriff but also Mitch's father. "I've been keeping an eye on him on this screen. So far it looks like they are doing everything by the book. I still want to stay and make sure everything is alright with Fred too. The last time I saw him I thought he was making his way toward this building, I'm sure he will be coming in at any minute. I will feel better when all of the procedural things are taken care of."

Mitch rubs his palms against the top of his thighs. "Do as you want but if there is anything that comes up that you think I need to know about, give me a call right away." He makes his way to his feet and looks down at the prisoner one more time. The man has a smug look on his face, with blood continuing to drip from his lower lip. A large knot has formed near his hairline and he most certainly has a broken nose. Mitch thinks about giving him one more solid left hand but thinks better of it and heads for the door.

"It was a pleasure meeting you Mr. Thompson. I hope I get to see you again real soon." The man speaks directly to Mitch for the first time and utters the words as if he was holding all of the cards instead of being tied to a chair and surrounded by federal agents. "Hopefully the next time we meet will be under different circumstances. Maybe there will be a few less members of law enforcement around."

Chapter 28

Once he reaches his truck, Mitch looks ahead at the park where he has spent the night. The Ferris Wheel looms large in the foreground and hovers high above everything else. He can still see the same Ferris Wheel car that he was stuck in while his father was being killed. He feels sorry for leaving the other two deputies, the only other remaining members of the Twisted Timbers police force, to have to deal with the questions that will come from the federal officers.

Judging by the colors of the morning sky, he can tell that the area will be hit with another spring shower at some point this afternoon. The low clouds move in fast from the west, off of the Pacific Ocean, and are becoming darker in color as they progress. With the turn of a key, the engine of his truck roars to life. Before he can even make it out of the parking lot, he is regretting leaving his father alone. He knows the agents will treat him with the same respect they would give one of their own, but it was his father. He breaks down in tears and buries his head in his hands. His forehead is resting on the steering wheel and the sobs are hard to stop.

He remains in that position for far too long, maybe even falling asleep for a minute or two. He is snapped out of it when he hears a familiar song on the radio. He wipes the salty tears from his eyes and puts the truck into gear. The truck makes a large circle in the gravel parking lot, dodging at least a dozen sedans that have made the journey from Portland. He points his vehicle toward the exit and gives the park one last look through the rear-view mirror. He watches as the Ferris Wheel begins light up and starts to rotate. He feels relief to know that the computer experts are making progress in their attempts to hack into the computer system and return the park to its rightful state. Mitch is grateful that except for his father, the other three members of the police department have made it through the night alive. He can just imagine the attention Fred will get at the bar when he begins telling the stories about this night.

As he steers his car toward the highway, he is happy to be finally putting the events that took place out of his mind. He reaches to turn up the radio when he suddenly hears a series of loud booming sounds behind him. He slams on the brakes of the truck and holds on tight as the blasts are strong enough to shake him in his seat. He checks his rear-view mirror again in just enough time to watch the Ferris Wheel tumble to its side and land in giant fire ball. Several more explosions can be heard off in the distance.

He thought the whole ordeal was over and he was about to be heading home. Now the crisp morning sky is filled with plumes of smoke and raging fires. His friends are still inside the park as well as countless federal agents. He ponders for a moment the severity of what he just witnessed, and momentarily thinks about driving away and letting the F.B.I. handle this part of the case on their own. He knows that his father wouldn't just run away from a problem like this, nor would he trust someone else to keep the folks in town safe from whatever could happen next.

Kevin M. Moehring

Chapter 29

It's hard for him to believe what he just saw, so he adjusts the rear-view mirror in hopes that he was mistaken. It never even occurred to him that he could just get out of the truck or turn it around to face the park. Now all he can see is large clouds of smoke and areas where flames shoot high into the air. Maybe he is just dreaming this. Maybe he fell asleep in his truck before he even started the ignition. A smaller explosive blast from somewhere deep inside the park lets him know that he is living this nightmare in real life. The small blasts continue for what seem like forever, each one leaving a new cloud of dark smoke to rise above the trees.

Mitch puts the truck in drive and spins it around. He drives right past where he was parked for most of the night and through the group of black sedans. The truck barely makes it through the large entrance gate to the park, but he doesn't slow down as he passes by the Ferris

Wheel and makes the turn toward where he left Agent Walker and more importantly, Stuart.

The entire office building is engulfed in flames and the roof no longer exists. Mitch slams on the brakes and the truck comes to a sliding stop just outside the entrance to the building. The fire is burning in a furious manner, making it hard for him to get anywhere close to the entrance. There are large piles of ashes laying on the ground a few feet from the building, small little fires are still burning through the ashes. When he realizes that these small fires are the remains of the agents who were trapped inside when the explosion ripped through the building, Mitch lets out a large stream of orange vomit. The smell of burning flesh is more than any man could handle, especially a small-town cop with just three years of experience.

He races back to the Ferris Wheel, coughing and gasping for clean air through the clouds of black smoke that seems to be everywhere. He races around the back of the ride, on the opposite side as where he passed by it earlier. The ride is not on fire, mainly due to the fact that it is constructed entirely out of steel. He finds two men leaning against the fence that separates the exit of the ride from the trees. The sight of someone who survived the blasts is a relief and he rushes to their side. When he notices that the one man is Fred, he is overcome with excitement.

"Hey Mitch, you look like you saw a ghost!" It is just like Fred to make light of the situation. The fact that he still has his sense of humor is the only sign needed to know that he is alright.

"I thought you were dead. We never saw you make it out of the ice cream building when it went up in flames. Stuart said he saw you wandering around on some of the cameras but after all of this, I didn't know if you were alive or not. What the hell happened here?" He has no idea who the second man is but judging from his attire, he assumes he is one of the federal officers.

"I'm not really sure. Just as I was about turn right and make my way to the main building, the whole ride started tumbling down. If this guy wouldn't have grabbed me when he did, it would have come down on top of me." Fred motions to the man sitting next to him, then points out the crumbled pile of steel that was once the most iconic ride in the park.

"Well we are lucky for that. Do you know what caused all of these explosions?" Mitch asks the question and takes his eyes from one man to the other. It didn't matter which one of them answered, as long as someone started telling him what happened.

"I have no clue. The sound of the ride coming down was so loud, when we got out from our hiding spot, all we could see was black smoke." Fred is the one who speaks first, not really giving an answer to the actual question.

"I'm Special Agent Michaels. The last thing I heard over the radio before everything went down was 'he's getting away and he's going to blow up the park.' I have no idea who he was talking about, but I would guess that it was the man that was tied up in the chair."

"I'm not sure how he would have been able to get out of the ropes, but I can't really think of anyone else who would be capable of doing this. I guess we need to walk the park and see how bad the damage is and if anyone is still alive." Mitch sticks out his hand to help Fred to his feet, then offers the same gesture to Officer Michaels.

As the three men start making their way through the park, they realize the damage is devastating. The roller coaster, which is completely wooden, is fully ablaze. Most of the water park is destroyed as is the area full of kids rides. It looks like multiple explosive devices were rigged to detonate at the same time, thus destroying most of the evidence as to what happened here. Hopefully the federal agents were able to salvage most of the evidence from the computer equipment before it was all lost.

Several agents make their way through the park and pass by the trio. Most of them have bewildered looks on their faces, skin covered in black smoke. "Agent Michaels, do you know if they had removed my father's body before the explosions went off?"

"Yes, they did. I watched them put him on the gurney and start wheeling him to the front of the park. I decided to walk along a different route back to the main building and that's when I saw Fred, walking in the opposite direction."

Mitch is relieved to know that even through all of this destruction, his father's body was not affected. "In the opposite direction? Fred, I thought you said you were making your way toward the building when the explosions happened?"

Fred stumbles across his words several times before finally being able to form a complete sentence. "I thought I was. A lot of things happened and I might not have been in a clear state of mind. It's just like me to be lost, isn't it?"

"Do you happen to know the whereabouts of the other deputy, Stuart Johnson?" Mitch accepts the explanation Fred gives him and fires off another question at Agent Michaels. "He was in the building when I left, and he was the only one in the room with the prisoner."

The man looks like he is deep in thought for a moment before he answers the question. "I had no idea where he was until I just heard the chatter on the radio. It looks like they found him and our suspect out in the parking lot. Mitch, the word is that your deputy was responsible for helping him escape."

Chapter 30

There's no way that Stuart would be willing to help that man escape. He couldn't be mixed up in all of this, could he? Mitch is running through every scenario in his mind as the three men make their way out to the parking lot of Graham Park. They hurry past the smoldering remains of the carousel that once held Stuart captive and Fred runs a little faster when they make it to the curled-up steel that was once the Ferris Wheel.

They dart past the entrance to the park and find several men gathered behind a black SUV in the parking lot. Stuart and Steven Graham are both lying on the ground, with hands behind their backs. Mitch walks right past Stuart and shoulders his way next to Agent Walker, who he had presumed was dead before seeing him here.

"Give me the rundown on what happened? One minute I'm getting in my truck and the very next minute, all hell breaks loose." His face is red, and his words are labored as he searches to catch his breath from the long sprint.

"There are still things we don't know. I was working with the guys in the server room when I heard a fellow agent call out that the suspect was getting away. I made it to the hallway in time to see them exit the building and a foot pursuit followed." Agent Walker pauses briefly and responds to someone over the radio. "Luckily whatever kind of self-destruct mechanism he had rigged had some sort of delay, otherwise there would be a few more agents that would have been lost. We managed to catch up to them out here, your deputy was easy to catch with his injured leg. The suspect was a little quicker, but we eventually got him."

"So, are you sure that Stuart was involved? There's no chance that there is a misunderstanding of some kind?" Mitch has known the accused officer for more than fifteen years and in all of that time there was no indication that he would be capable of assisting in something like this.

"I don't think he was in on it from the beginning, but he definitely had something to do with the suspect being released and allowing him to trigger the explosives. We were able to tap into the live feeds from the cameras before the blasts knocked everything offline. Most of the actual video feeds were being saved offsite, meaning there was no damage to them from the explosions. Once we figure out the severity of the damage and the number of agents we lost, we will go over the video. You are more than welcome to be there for that, and for the interrogation of your deputy, if you'd like."

Mitch paces around the area and refuses to look down at his friend. The thought that Stuart is somehow responsible for the destruction here in unfathomable. He hated violence and had a pension for finding a way of excusing himself before a situation became to hairy. This is not the Stuart that has been a member of the Twisted Timbers Police Department for over a decade.

"I would appreciate that, thank you. I guess I will bypass the rest of the formalities and meet you back at the station. Do you want me to transport him?"

"That won't be necessary. He is the custody of the F.B.I. and policy dictates that one of ours must transport him. I appreciate the help and the use of your facilities. I will send some agents over there right away to make sure we have things in order before I get there." Agent Walker speaks to Mitch as if they are co-workers, which is the complete opposite of how he usually gets spoken to by federal agents.

"It's not a problem and thank you for getting your guys here so quickly. I'll see you back in town." Mitch turns and walks away from the gathering of men, kicking at the loose rocks in the gravel as he heads toward his truck. His head is hung low until he reaches the side of the ambulance that holds the body of his father. He places his right hand on the back door of the ambulance and spends a moment in deep reflection before finishing with a prayer. He notices that Fred is making his way to his own vehicle and rushes over to meet him.

"Hey Mitch, do you believe what they are saying? It just doesn't sound like Stuart to me." Fred looks rough and tired. His uniform is no longer tucked in at the waist, something the sheriff would have pointed out immediately.

"I don't know what to think but that's what they are saying. I'm holding judgement until we get back and can see the video. You heading back to the station?"

"Yeah, they want me to give them my story as to how things went down. Want me to grab some food on the way?" If there is one thing that Fred enjoyed more than chasing women, it was a food.

"Sure, that would be great. Fred, make sure you don't talk to anyone about this until we know what's going on. We don't need the entire town in a panic before we have the facts." Mitch is aware of the fact that with the sheriff being dead, someone is going to have to step up and think about what is best for the town on a daily basis.

"No problem Mitch, but if I hadn't known any better, I would have guessed those words had come right out of the sheriff's mouth. I don't think I had a chance to tell you, and I'm sure you already know, but I'm really sorry for your loss. The town will not be the same without your father."

Kevin M. Moehring

Chapter 31

The ride back to town is a familiar one but today the winding road seems to go by in a blur. The hills don't seem so steep and the sharp curves are far less intimidating. Since leaving Graham Park, Mitch has been unable to focus on anything in front of him. Thoughts of his father, the headless man on the roller coaster and the tumbling Ferris Wheel cycle through his mind as if they are on a constant loop. Things like this just don't happen in his small town, at least they didn't before last night. There is no telling how the town council will react once they find out what has happened, but he feels confident that he did everything in his power to keep the town safe.

He turns off of the highway and down the two-lane road at the center of town. The police station sits behind the only grocery store in town and about two blocks from Mitch's tiny apartment. He parks his truck in one of the empty spots in the rear of the building and heads inside. He is greeted by Lucille Pennington, the receptionist that has worked at the office longer than anyone else had, including Sheriff Thompson.

"Hey Mitch, good morning. There's some coffee in the back. It looks like you had a long night." Her upbeat personality is the last thing Mitch wants to hear right now.

"You have no idea and thanks for the coffee. Do you always work on Sundays?" This is the first time Mitch can remember being at the office on a Sunday when it wasn't tourist season, so he has no idea if Lucille is normally here or not.

"Not normally, but the sheriff wanted me to come in and get his files in order. Every election year he gets worried that someone will beat him out, even though he usually runs uncontested. He makes me get things in order just in case." She is holding a large stack of manila folders and has just left the tiny office that belonged to his father.

"Well, I don't think you need to worry about the election this year or getting his personal files together. He passed away last night." He is going to have to get used to saying these words but right now they only partially come out through his quivering lower lip.

"What! What are you talking about?" Lucille normally has a perfectly elegant voice, one that has been formed over many years of answering phones. She now speaks in a loud squeal that Mitch has never heard come out of her mouth. "Please tell me you're joking. Oh, dear Lord, this is not something you joke about young man."

"Lucille, I wish I was joking. There was a lot of things that happened last night, you will find out all the details when the feds get here. Be prepared for it to be a lot more chaotic in here than we're all used to." Mitch opens the door to his father's office and looks inside, decides he's not quite ready to go in and goes back to the side of Lucille's desk. "We need to clear out the conference room, I'm sure they are going to need it. Is the one cell still full of boxes?"

"I believe so. Are we going to need both cells?" The old lady is now standing and tidying up the space, much how women do when they find out they were having unexpected company. "It shouldn't be too hard to get the boxes out of there."

"Lucille, relax. I don't care what this place looks like or that there's dust on things. You have no idea the severity of the events of last night. We are going to need that extra cell though. I doubt Agent Walker will want to put Stuart into the same cell as Steven Graham."

"Wait, why in the world would they put Officer Johnson in a cell?"

Chapter 32

Lucille has been running around the office trying to clear out the boxes from the second cell. Mitch tried to explain to her what had happened last night, but he only got as far as telling her about the Ferris Wheel before the federal agents started coming in. From the moment they got there, they took over the small police station. Guys with wind breakers with F.B.I. printed in large yellow letters on the back, scurry around the rooms. They carry in loads of equipment that causes Mitch to look out of the window to see how big of a truck they brought to get all of this stuff here from Portland.

It isn't too much longer before Agent Michaels comes in, holding tightly to the arm of Stuart Johnson. The once proud officer now walks through the station with his head hung low and refusing to make eye contact with anyone. When the agent escorting him stops to speak to another agent, Stuart looks up and looks directly into the eyes of Mitch. Stuart acts like he is going to say something to Mitch but is having a tough time finding the right words. The two men stare at each other without saying a word, both knowing that things are going to get very complicated, very quickly.

Lucille shows Agent Michaels the way to the holding cells as Mitch follows them with his eyes. Shortly after, a large swarm of agents enter through the back door. Agent Walker can be seen pushing Steven Graham in the middle of the group as they disappear to the holding area. Mitch is quick to follow the group of men, wanting to be a part of whatever is happening in his police station.

No sooner had Mitch made it to where the cells are that the group has turned around and is heading back down the same corridor. He holds the door and the five men shuffle through, with Walker leading the way. Mitch follows behind, like a third wheel on a dinner date, and tries to listen closely to everything that comes out of Walker's mouth. The agent in charge speaks in a definitive tone that lets the others know that he has things under control. Men are frantically moving around the main room, setting up monitors and plugging in laptops.

There has never been so much activity in this small office and Mitch is already dreading the coming days.

While he is sitting down at his desk, slowly writing down the events of the night on a notepad, he is interrupted by the smell of warm food. He looks up to find Fred standing in front of his desk with two large bags from the diner down the road. It has been a long night and an even longer morning. This is the first time he has even thought about food since he started his shift yesterday.

"Sit down Fred, we can eat together. I was working on writing down my story before I forget anything, and trying to stay out of the way." He clears a few files from his desk so there is room for both men to eat comfortably. "Everything has happened so quickly that I haven't even thought about food."

Fred rolls the office chair from his desk over and sits on the opposite side. "I guess I should write down my side of the story too, but it's going to take a really long time before I forget anything about last night."

"Yeah, you got that right. I still can't believe Stuart would let the man out. He must not have known the park was rigged with explosives." He takes a long look inside the foam container. He had expected to see breakfast food but when he checks the clock and realizes it's a little past noon, the hamburger makes more sense.

"I hope the hamburger is alright, I didn't really know what to get you." Fred has already begun to cover his french fries using the little packets of ketchup that restaurants hand out.

"It's perfect, thanks. Hey, now that we're alone, I want to ask you what happened to you when you made it out of the fire? I know Stuart saw you on the camera a few times, but I have no idea what kind of experiences you had. Did you run into the sheriff at all before he was killed?" He shoves a few french fries into his mouth and looks across at what is now the only other member of the small-town police force.

"I didn't see much, I tried to stay hidden as best that I could. I've been meaning to ask you something. Are you upset with me? The last time we talked we were having the disagreement in the shack before it went up in flames. Is that why you left me in there and took off with Stuart?"

Mitch pauses with his mouth on the hamburger. He had not even thought to be resentful toward Fred. "I am not upset with you at all. I left you there so that I could get Stuart out of the building before it all came down on top of us. I assumed you were going to be right behind us but then I never saw you again. There are several things I regret from last night, mainly not being able to save my father, but leaving you behind is not one of them. I knew you would do what you had to in order to survive. I am just thankful that you were able to escape the blaze and survive without too much trouble."

"If you say so. I just don't want there to be any tension between us moving forward. It looks like we are about all that is left of the cops in this town." Fred doesn't notice the spot of mustard that remains on his lip as he talks but he manages to clean it off with a firm swipe of a napkin.

"And since you're the senior member, I guess that makes you the acting sheriff." It hadn't occurred to Mitch that this fact would not have registered right away with Fred. The look of surprise in his eyes makes Mitch think that he is already getting nervous about having to fill the shoes of the senior Thompson.

"Oh shit! I didn't even think about it. I have to deal with all of this now. These agents are going to be all

over the place for a while, I'm not sure I can handle it."
He drops his food in disgust, obviously not happy after
learning of his new title. He pushes the container away
and folds his arms, his face twisted into a pout.

"They will be here for a while, that's for sure. All
you can do is answer their questions honestly, give them
all the help they need and hopefully they will be out of
our hair soon enough. It won't be long until things are
back to normal around here." Mitch throws the last bite
of his hamburger into his mouth, takes a long drink of
the soda that came with the food. It was probably
because he hadn't eaten in so long, but he thinks that may
have been the best meal he has eaten in several years.

"That's easy for you to say. You're not the man
that has to fill the shoes of the biggest legend in town. It
would be far easier for you to take over as sheriff because
you're his son. The people here already consider me a
joke of an officer." Fred closes the container and tosses
it into the nearby garbage can.

"You'll do fine. People in this town are going to
be grateful that we did our job to the best of our ability.
They aren't going to ask you to be like him." Before
Mitch can finish talking and fully convince Fred that

everything is going to be alright, they are summoned to the conference room. Apparently, they have the video feed from the park and Walker wants them both there to add their insight.

"Mitch, this is going to be weird, watching everything that happened last night on a television screen like it was a movie," Fred says as the two men walk down the hallway to the conference room.

"It's going to very different, but I need to know what happened. If Stuart really set that man free and allowed him to fire off the explosives, then I need to see it with my own eyes." They match each other with their steps, walking toward the conference room.

They take the next few steps in silence and just as the reach the door, Fred speaks up. "It's not reliving the events from last night that worries me. It's actually finding out the truth about Stuart that I'm afraid of."

Kevin M. Moehring

Chapter 33

There is a large gathering of suits all piled into the small conference room. Some of the men Mitch can recognize from the parking lot of Graham Park, while others just seem to have magically appeared. Agent Walker is at the front of the room with his back to everyone else. He is staring at the large flat screen television that has somehow been mounted on the wall. The frame on the screen has been paused but you can see the Ferris Wheel is dark and the sun is beginning to set.

Agent Walker speaks to the only guy in the room who is not in uniform or wearing a suit coat. This man is seated at a desk in the corner of the room with several computers in front of him. He frantically taps away at the keyboard, and pauses briefly to answer the agent in charge before tapping away again. Mitch and Fred find seats in the back corner and try to remain invisible to the feds.

"Now that we are all here, let's get started." Agent Walker stands in front of the room and addresses his colleagues. He makes certain to give Mitch and Fred the eye contact to acknowledge they are present. "We have been able to piece together as much footage from last night as we could, gathering feeds from several different sites that were streaming the event. From these feeds we can almost figure out everything that happened, but there are still a few things that we don't know and will require a little more time to process. We are going to fast forward through much of the night at this point, only really paying attention to the details needed to piece together a timeline. The only real mystery is how the suspect escaped and was able to set off the explosives."

"Are we firm in the belief that the local officer assisted him?" Mitch snaps his head to his right to see the voice come from an overweight agent who he had not yet seen. "Seems to me that there is really no other explanation."

"I want us to look at the whole evening with an open mind. I'm going to show all of the video feed we have from the time it started, and the wagering began, until the time the explosions happened." Walker whispers something to the agent with the computers before turning back to the group. "We weren't there so none of us know what really happened, with the exception of the two officers seated in the back of the room." Agent Walker pauses long enough for the whole room to turn and look at the men in question before speaking again. "I've only seen bits and pieces of the footage, so I am going to be forming my opinions and theories along with the rest of you."

Mitch and Fred give each other a look that let each other know that they are not looking forward to what is about to be played on the screen. An agent heads for the door and turns off the overhead lights and Agent Walker takes his seat as the video starts to play.

The image of the Ferris Wheel that has been paused on the large screen begins to darken and a large graphic pops in front of it. In bold red letters, like the title screen of a movie, *'Death Game XII'* appears. The title screen fades away and is soon replaced with the words *'The Crew'* at the top. Under these words are six pictures, all matching the faces that were on the pieces of paper that were found in the park and are now logged as evidence. Under each picture is the opening odds for all of the participants, with the patriotic American being the hands down favorite to win.

The last of the crew members faces leaves the screen just as the bright lights of the Ferris Wheel come to life. The large metal ride begins to rotate around the center point. The whole production of the video is very high quality, resembling any number of reality shows that are put on television each year. Mitch flashes back to rolling into the parking lot and seeing this exact image. He remembers the comedy his fellow officers found when he first told them what he saw and how he doubts either of them find it funny now.

The serenity of watching the wheel move around and around is quickly replaced by the loud clattering of the *Wood Splitter* racing down one of its steep hills. The footage doesn't show how the man came to be trapped inside the passenger car, but it does catch the moment that Roger Sheffield lost his head. The video is grainy and hard to decipher who accomplished the beheading, but it must have been the Russian, Vladimir Strotsky, since he was killed with the head in his bag. At the exact moment of the killing, the dollar figure under his picture on the screen increased. The gruesome sight of the man swinging the machete at the helpless victim made some of the agents in the room turn their heads, especially during the scene when the killer holds the head high in the air and smiles like he was an important trophy.

Fred shifts in his seat unknowingly, making it hard for Mitch to pay attention and try to figure out anything about the night that he didn't already know. The video shifts to the carousel and Stuart is seen on-screen for the first time. The room breaks into laughter at the sight of the officer stumbling over the metal barricades before making his way to the ride. Just as he described, Stuart gets startled by something and practically dives into the small room behind one of the mirrors. Moments later the ride lights up and begins to spin around. The animals begin to dance along to the calypso music, which can also be heard on the video.

As the ride begins to speed up, much faster than it would normally rotate, a dark figure can be seen leaving the ride and disappearing in the bushes. Mitch guesses this is the person responsible for writing the message on the mirror that Stuart found when the ride stopped moving. Once again, the video becomes very dark and three fresh faces are posted on the side, along with the other members of *'The Crew'*. Now the three deputies of the Twisted Timber Police Department are listed alongside the South American mercenary and the American sniper.

Fred is now sweating through his shirt, moving in his chair like a school kid who is in dire need of a trip to the restroom. "Are you alright? I've never seen you act like this," Mitch whispers to him.

"I'm fine. It's just hard to watch everything again. I was there and lived it firsthand." The nervous man is now rubbing his palms along his thighs, trying to dry the moisture that has formed.

"We were both there, but this is the best way to figure out what really happened. This is the best way to clear our friend's name." His attention is drawn back to the television as the shot rang out and he watches his friend hit the concrete ground below. His sees himself on the screen, as he rushes out to pick up Stuart and disappear inside the ice cream shack.

Once all three men are inside of the building another shadowy figure appears. It could be the same person but the quality of the video and the lack of lighting in the area makes it hard to determine. The person is seen covering the building in a liquid and lighting it on fire. Soon the screen is bright as the flames engulf the structure and the two men come out, racing for the security of the woods.

Mitch continues to stare at the screen intently, waiting to see how Fred was able to make it out. He looks at the man sitting next to him, who now has his face in his hands, refusing to watch the events unfold. A single person runs back into the building and comes out carrying someone, most certainly Fred.

"Pause it right there and see if we can enhance the image. There should be enough light from the fire, so we can make out who is carrying the body from the fire." Agent Walker's voice breaks through the silence of the room as he points to the computer expert.

"We should be able to, but it would mean I have to stop playing the video for about an hour until we figure it out. I'll make a note of the frame you want enhanced and as soon as we've ran the feed in its entirety, I'll go back and enhance this image." The computer guy makes a few strokes on the keyboard and the video begins to play once again.

"Who was that? Who carried you out of there?" Mitch is once again talking to Fred in a quiet tone so that his words cannot be heard from the dozen federal agents in the room.

"I don't know. Let's just watch this thing so we can get out of here." He is apparently agitated with the whole situation, much like Mitch is. It has been a long night for everyone involved and the lack of sleep is starting to play on their nerves.

"Just sit there patiently, I'm not sure I want to be here and watch my father being killed any more than you do. It's just something we have to deal with." The two men nod at each other and return their sights back to the video on the screen.

The room sits silently as they watch Stuart kill the Colombian in the woods and watch as the large Kenyan gets the upper hand on the American and ties him to the back side of the Ferris Wheel. Much of it is hard to make out, due to the lack of lighting, but the computer guy assures Agent Walker that he will be able to clean it all up if he is given a few hours.

Suddenly the screen is bright and the suspect, Mr. Graham, is seated near a row of computer screens. The entire room leans in to get a closer look, knowing that what they are seeing is the beginning of the explanation to how the suspect escaped. Sheriff Thompson barges into the room from behind the suspect and lets him have it with a few quick jabs that stun the man. He throws him out of his seat and up against the wall where he pats the man down before tossing him back into his chair. The size difference between Steven Graham and the sheriff is noticeable as he treats the suspect like he is a little kid. The sheriff disappears from frame for a few seconds before returning to the room with rope and duct tape.

Once the man has been secured, the sheriff has a look around the room and pushes the man, chair and all down the hallway to the room next door. The agents all sigh as soon as they realize that the smoking gun they were hoping to find, hasn't been found just yet. The video continues to play and show the rest of the events of the night. The fight to free the soldier from the Ferris Wheel, Sheriff Thompson leaving in a mad dash for the water park once he hears that there is a body down there and the fight between Fred and the Japanese karate expert.

The screen now splits into two separate images, one follows Mitch as he makes his way back to the office building, after he found his father dead on the pathway. The second feed shows what is going on inside the rooms of the office building. The agents scurrying through the place like little mice hunting for the last morsel of cheese. Most eyes in the conference room are focused on the right side of the screen, looking for any scrap of evidence that they could have missed.

Once all parties are inside the same building, the feed returns to just one image. Most of the federal agents are huddled inside the room with all of the computer equipment with Stuart still sitting in the chair in front of the monitors. Mitch is standing in front of Mr. Graham, obviously asking him questions about what has happened. The screen shows Agent Walker enter the room and speak directly to Mitch, and if he remembers correctly, this is when the agent told him to go home and get some sleep.

Not long after Mitch leaves the building and makes his way to his truck, Fred is seen entering the room where the suspect has been tied up. The conference room remains quiet and waits to see how the man frees himself from the ropes. Mitch is watching the screen like everyone else, but he is also going back through his mind to remember the events exactly as they happened. He remembers seeing Fred in the parking lot shortly after he left the park. He even vaguely remembers him saying something about getting food, but he can't remember if that took place before or after the blasts.

On the screen, the words cannot be heard but there is an extensive dialogue between Fred Donovan and Steven Graham. It continues for several minutes until Fred walks over to the man, reaches into his pocket and hands the prisoner a metallic object. Fred practically runs out of the room after giving the man whatever the object is. A few heads in the conference room turn toward the deputy before returning their gaze to the screen.

No sooner had Fred left the room and the prisoner is using the object to cut through the ropes that bind him. It takes him several minutes to cut through the ropes until he is completely free. He rises to his feet and tries to inch his way to the doorway without rising suspicion. He puts his head out to peek around the corner and when he thinks the coast is clear he moves rapidly out of the building. The camera follows him as he makes his way along the hallway and outside of the building.

A soft voice can be heard in the background as Steven Graham makes his way to the parking lot in an attempt to flee the scene. The camera angle changes again and everyone is watching Stuart, with his injured leg, hobble after the man. He is in agony with every step, but he is the only one who sees that the man is getting away.

"Stop! I've seen enough. We obviously have the wrong deputy in custody," barks Agent Walker. As if on cue, the entire room turns to face Mitch and the empty chair that is next to him. Everyone was so focused on what was happening on the screen that they hadn't seen Fred exit the room. Even Mitch didn't know he had left and Fred would have had to walk right in front of him in order to leave the room.

Voices ring out from all corners of the room. Questions are being asked about how long Fred had been gone and making accusations that Mitch had to know when he left. One agent even stands up and says that he saw the two men whispering throughout the video. Mitch is as stunned as anyone else in the room. While all of the agents are speaking at once, Mitch just stands up and exits the room quietly. Once again it is highly unlikely that any of the agents even noticed that he has left. He begins walking down the long corridor that leads to the holding cells. Halfway down the hallway he is stopped by the voice of Agent Walker behind him.

"Where do you think you are going?" Walker is almost in a sprint until he sees that Mitch has stopped and turned to the sound of his voice.

"Well it's obvious, isn't it? We have a suspect at large and the only other deputy I have left in this town is trapped in a prison cell, wrongly accused I might add."

"I agree he is innocent, but you have to look at it from our side. He was seen fleeing the building with Mr. Graham. It seemed likely that he was the one who freed the man from the ropes and helped him escape."

"Did you bother to ask him what his side of the story was?" Mitch is practically yelling at the federal officer.

"Shortly after we apprehended the two, the fireworks went off. It was total chaos and we didn't have much of a chance. That is why we brought them here, so we could sort things out. It's standard operating procedure in times like these to arrest the most likely suspects and sort out the details when things have become much calmer."

"Well we have sorted things out. The man you want has escaped and nobody knows him or this town like Stuart and myself. I am going to free my fellow deputy and we are going to bring in Fred. You lost good men today and these agents have assuredly lost friends. I don't want your guys to get a little happy on the trigger finger." Mitch turns and heads away from the agent as if there was nothing that could be done to stop him.

"Mitch my computer guy just came over the radio. He said he was able to clear up some more of the feed. There is something else you need to know about our fugitive. He says it was Officer Donovan that killed your father. I'm sorry."

Chapter 34

With a firm turn of the solid brass key, Mitch opens the door to the holding cell. He steps in and looks at his friend and fellow officer, who looks relieved to see that it is Mitch who has come to see him. The medics at the scene bandaged his leg and gave him some pain medicine, which seems to have worn off given the look on his face when he tries to stand up.

"Boy am I glad to see you. What are they accusing me of? All I remember is being told to go and get some rest then seeing Steven Graham run through the parking lot. I tried to catch up to him, but I only had one good leg. Then the next thing I know, I'm being tackled by several guys and handcuffed." Stuart must have been practicing his story while he has been in this cell.

"Calm down Stu, the truth has come out and I'm here to let you out. You did nothing wrong at all. In fact,

I might have to talk to the mayor about getting you some sort of recommendation." Mitch gives him a wink of confidence while swinging open the iron door.

"Wait, I'm free to go? I thought they said I was going to fry for helping with the explosions." The look of confusion on his face is about to get far worse when he hears the next part of what Mitch has to say.

"We can talk about it in the truck. Right now, we have to go find Fred. We watched the video from the park and he is the one who helped Steven Graham escape. When we went to arrest him, he had somehow sneaked out. I want us to find him before the feds do. That is the only way we know that he will be brought in safely."

"Fred is involved? There is no way that's possible. Where do you think he went?" Stuart is talking like a man who has had his whole life turned inside and out over the course of the last twelve hours.

"If you were Fred, where would you go?" He asks the question as the two men enter the office area and head for the door to the outside. Fred shields his eyes from the bright afternoon sun as he gets into the passenger seat of the truck.

"If I know Fred, he is over at the bar. I thought he would be excited to reap the benefits of actually being involved in a good police case. I never thought he would put himself in the middle of it." Stuart is still a little confused over the happenings of the last few hours.

"Then we start at The Bottom Dollar and go from there. I don't know what happened when he was left alone with Steven Graham, but he definitely gave him the knife he used to cut the ropes free." The ride to the bar is a short one, just down Main Street to the corner of Maple. He finds a spot just off the street and the two men make their way inside.

The Bottom Dollar is the only bar in town that is open year-round. It has been around for longer than anyone can remember, and the odor of stale beer and warped wooden floor boards fills the air. Mitch has been in the place a time or two but not nearly enough times to be considered a regular. Fred on the other hand, practically has a bar stool with his name on it.

The two deputies make their way around the long bar, dodging peanut shells on the floor to try not to draw attention to themselves. Sitting on the far corner of the room, with a half full mug of beer and an empty shot glass in front of him, sits Fred Donovan. He doesn't raise his head to look at them, even though it was hard to imagine that he didn't know that they were there. The large bell on the inside of the door was a sure giveaway that someone had entered, and not too many people come into the bar on a Sunday afternoon.

Mitch gives a hand signal to Stuart and they sit at the two open stools on either side of him. Fred stares blankly in front of him, at the rows of liquor bottles that line the wall behind the bar. He knows they are there, but right now he is more worried about being able to finish his drink. He motions for the bartender, a portly lady in her mid-forties who is trying to look fashionable in clothes that don't really fit, and she fills his shot glass again. He downs the drink with ease, slams the empty glass to the table and looks at Mitch.

"Hey Fred, what in the world were you thinking?" Mitch didn't have much time to role play how he expected this conversation to go but now that they are here he is unsatisfied with how he started the questioning. He remembers the dozens of movies his father would watch, admiring how cool and collected the detectives would be when questioning a suspect. Now that he is actually in a similar position, his words come out more like a kid trying to ask a girl out to prom.

"Cecilia, another beer please." Fred is still finding it hard to look at either of the men on his sides but remains focused on the drinks being poured for him. "I don't know what I was thinking. That man pulled me from that burning building. He told me things were probably going to get hairy and he was right. He promised to make me a very rich man if I helped him make it out of the park safely."

"Money? You did all of this for money? Money is a good thing, but I don't think there is enough money in the world that would make me want to kill a building full of federal officers." Mitch reaches into the bowl of nuts and cracks a few of the shells. He thinks if he tosses a few into his mouth it may give the impression that he is not furious at the moment.

"I had no idea that was going to happen. He must have had everything rigged to blow at a certain time. If I would have known his entire plan, I never would have gone along with it. All he told me was the minute he made it out of Graham Park, he would make sure I would never have to work again."

"Did he tell you that you had to kill my father. Did he tell you that he would make you filthy rich and all you had to do was kill the sheriff?" The blood has rushed to Mitch's face and the tension between the two men now burns brighter than the neon beer sign on the wall behind them. Stuart can feel the intensity and leaves his stool to stand in between the men but stays a few feet behind them.

"We both know that if the sheriff is on the case, then the chances of Steven Graham getting out of the park would have been much worse. I did what I needed to do to accomplish the task at hand, just like the good sheriff has taught me over the years." Another long drink out of his beer mug and Fred is ready for another shot of whiskey. "I didn't want to kill your father, but he was going to ruin the plan."

"So you just walked up to him and stabbed him? You just took the life of one of the finest men this town has ever seen, all in an attempt to get rich. He treated you like a son."

"That's not how it went down at all. He was racing across the park and I walked in front of him and stopped him. We talked for a bit and then he said he had

Steven Graham tied up in the office building. That's when I decided that in order to make sure I got paid, I had to kill the sheriff." He says the words as if he doesn't have a care in the world or an ounce of remorse. "I told him I was happy to see him and that I knew it would all be over with soon since he was on the case. I leaned in to give him a hug and stabbed him with the small sword I got when I choked out the Japanese guy."

Mitch leans back into his bar stool and reaches into his coat pocket. "Now that I have your taped confession, I guess the only thing left to do is to put the cuffs on you. I really didn't think it would be this easy to get the information out of you." He lays the metal tape recorder on the bar and presses the stop button. He calls for Cecilia who rushes right over to them, "I think I'm ready for a drink now."

Kevin M. Moehring

Chapter 35

The idea to run the tape recorder was a brilliant move and one that his father would have been proud of. Having to arrest a man he worked side by side with for the last few years is not something Mitch wants to ever repeat again. Fred was not able to keep up his machismo persona once he realized that it was all over and there was no way for him to get out of this bar. The sound of the sirens outside let him know that the federal agents had surrounded the place and he was heavily outnumbered.

Stuart raced out of the bar once he realized the agents had shown up. He is able to hold them at bay long enough for Mitch to do a thorough pat down and confiscate the police issued revolver from Fred. It is hard to see a once proud man, who took pride in being the toughest man in the room, now broken and sobbing like a child. Mitch lets him finish one more shot, which he follows with the remainder of the beer in his mug. When he places the glass back on the bar, Mitch pulls his arms behind his back and places the handcuffs on him, making sure to not tighten them too tight. It was in everyone's best interest to keep Fred thinking that it was a friend who was bringing him in.

The few steps it takes to walk toward the door seem to take much longer than they would under normal circumstances. The guilty man has his head hung in shame as Mitch leads him toward the front door. Once they exit the building, they are practically crushed by the herd of federal agents who have gathered outside. Luckily, due to the remoteness of the small town, there is no media to worry about. Mitch continues to usher his prisoner through the crowd, leading him by the arm as they make their way to the truck parked nearby.

Fred is more than happy to disappear inside the passenger side of the truck. As Mitch closes the door and begins to head to the driver's side, he is face to face with an angry looking Agent Walker. He is obviously upset that Mitch was able to find and arrest the wanted man so quickly. Before the two men could have a heated exchange, Stuart steps between them and begins to usher the federal agent away from the truck. The interference is enough of a distraction to allow Mitch to fire the truck up and head away from the gathered mass of law enforcement that has surrounded the bar.

They head straight to the police station and not a single word is said between the two men. The low grumble of the engine is the only noise that breaks through the intensity between a murderer and the son of the man he killed. Mitch takes up several parking spots as he parks the truck right in front of the main door to the station. He races around and opens the passenger door and reaches in to help Fred out. A few short steps later and they are inside the building and making their way to the holding cells when the rush of agents begin to make their way back from the bar.

The loud clank of the metal door closing brings an end to the short search for the former officer. He sticks his hands between the bars and allows Mitch to remove the cuffs. He turns back to his friend and finally looks him in the face. "I'm sorry Mitch. I know there isn't much I can do that will change anything, but I need you to know that I am sorry."

Mitch can hear the footsteps coming down the hallway and he knows his time alone with Fred will soon be over. He has been lucky thus far, the F.B.I. is famous for taking over investigations and making sure the local police force has nothing to do with it. In this case, he has been very involved in the entire investigation. Even though he didn't give Agent Walker much of a choice, he was able to bring in the suspect and lock him in the cell without assistance from the feds.

He doesn't respond to the words from Fred. Instead, he turns and begins to head back down the corridor to the central office. He stops as soon as he passes the cell that still holds Steven Graham. The mastermind of the entire series of events that led to several men losing their life, sits quietly on the bed and smiles out at Mitch. The coldness in his eyes infuriates the officer. How can a person be so obsessed with money that they are willing to kill anyone they encounter?

"Stop! Mitch, I really need to know what you're thinking. I didn't intend to kill anyone." The words break the stare between Mitch and Steven Graham. Reluctantly Mitch returns to the door of Fred's cell. "All I wanted to do was to make a little money and get out of this awful town."

"Fred, I don't really care about what you were thinking. I don't really know what to think about any of this. I thought you were a friend and never in my wildest dreams did I think you would ever be capable of something like this." Mitch is shouting now, much as he remembers his father doing whenever Mitch had done something wrong as a child.

"I understand what you are saying but I hope that in the future you will be able to forgive me. I am not a killer."

"Forgive you? Right now, I want to reach through these bars and choke the life out of you." His complexion has turned a bright shade of red. The rush of frustration and anger has finally boiled over to the point where he is ready to lash out at Fred. "You make a decision that you wanted the money and you were willing to do anything to get it. You say you are not a killer, but you looked my father right in the eye before you stabbed him. That makes you the worst kind of killer. You handed the lunatic in the other cell a knife that allowed him to escape, moments before the explosions. I have no idea how many lives were lost as a result of that. Now you tell me you are not a killer and you hope I can forgive you? Listen closely to what I am saying. I hope you get everything that is coming to you. I am going to be at every court appearance you make, and I am going to make sure that they throw the book at you. I want you to see my face every time you wake up in the morning and every night before you go to sleep. I want you to remember me in the last moments before you burn in hell."

He needed to get those words out and he needed Fred to know his thoughts. He turns away from his former friend and walks away silently. He is met in the hallway by Agent Walker, who has apparently been listening to the verbal tirade. Mitch hands him the tape recorder that caught Fred's confession before the two men share a knowing nod and make their way past each other without speaking.

The shuffling of agents in the office makes it difficult for Mitch to make his way out of the station. He stopped long enough to give Stuart a grin and a nod of approval before making it down the steps and outside to his truck. Once in the driver's seat, he pauses long enough to allow the fire in his body to die down. It has been a very long and confusing day. One that started like it would be just another calm, early spring day. It was twenty-four hours ago when this whole thing began when he rolled into the parking lot of Graham Park. He turns the key in the ignition and starts the lonely drive home to his apartment.

Kevin M. Moehring

Chapter 36

It has been three days since the conclusion of the events that happened at Graham Park. The F.B.I. has pretty much taken over the police station in that time but things are wrapping up and the agents that are still in town have become scarce. Mitch has stepped away from the investigation almost completely, allowing Agent Walker to have complete control. Today is also the day that the body of Sheriff Thompson will be laid to rest.

As expected with a case of this magnitude, the national media has ascended on the small town of Twisted Timbers. Normally at this time of year, the streets of town would be nearly empty at all times of the day. Now there is a steady stream of news vans entering and leaving town. Agent Walker has become a hit with the reporters and has been seen on television sets across the country for the last few days.

Mitch has had numerous requests for interviews but has turned them all down. The town has come together and shown unbelievable support for him on the loss of his father. The mayor of the town quickly named Mitch the new sheriff, only after making sure that Stuart wanted nothing to do with the title. He was sworn in at a private ceremony that was conducted at City Hall the night after he arrested Fred at the bar.

Mitch is currently in his dress uniform, attending a final briefing being led by Agent Walker. This meeting is basically a summary of everything they have been able to find out about the case in the preceding days. The bodies of all the participants in the game, except for that of Jesse Meyer, have already been transported to Portland for autopsies. The final death toll has been listed as thirteen people, five of the killers, the sheriff and seven federal officers who were killed in the series of explosions that ripped through the park.

Most of the information that is being supplied has been a result of the demanding work of the computer staff. They have been able to find out that the explosives were set on a timer and did not need to be remotely triggered. No matter what happened, there would have been no way for anyone to stop the explosions from happening. The grand total of money that was wagered and lost on the event totaled just over fifty million dollars. That figure does not include the nearly forty million dollars that was collected as a subscription fee in order to just watch the streaming video. Agent Walker explains that he has already been in talks with the State Attorney's Office about making sure that most of the recovered funds are used to rebuild the park and cover funeral expenses for the fallen men.

An agent on the left side of the table asks for an update on the missing killer, the former Army Ranger. Agent Walker is quick to point out that they have several men working on the identity and location of the man but have not been able to make much progress, as of yet. They have checked with the military and the name of Jesse Meyer is not listed as ever being an active member. The meeting ends without much more information being shared than anyone in the country could read about in their morning paper.

Stuart Johnson is leaning against his truck when Mitch walks out of the police station. He has been insistent upon trying to help make the new sheriff overcome the grief of losing his father. They ride to the cemetery together and Mitch does his best to avoid the small talk. Today will mark the conclusion to the two biggest things that have happened to him so far during his adult life. The death of his father will rest heavier on his mind than anything that happened at the park.

It looks like the entire town has shown up to say their final goodbyes to Sheriff Thompson. He was loved in the town and was a face that everyone knew. Most of the people who had known him all their life are here to show their support. Mitch walks slowly through the rows of chairs, shaking hands and getting hugs from several people who he could not name. It takes far too long for him to reach the only empty seat next to the grave. He sits down and nods to the priest that he can begin the service.

Most of the normal passages were read from the Bible and the priest spoke fondly of the departed. Mitch daydreams during most of the funeral, choosing to reminisce about the good times he spent with his father, rather than have someone tell him how good of a man he was. When the final words are spoken, and the men begin throwing dirt on top of the grave, Mitch stands and again is met with handshakes and hugs from strangers. He has never seen so many grown men crying in one place before. He has not yet been able to shed a single tear over his father's death, exactly how Bill Thompson would have wanted him to mourn.

He is surprised to see that the few federal agents that are still in town have made an appearance and have taken their place in line to give Mitch their condolences. Agent Walker is the last of these agents and makes sure to remind him that if there is anything he can do to help him out, to let him know. Walker has already agreed to upgrade several of the computers in the police station, to at least get the town into the twenty-first century.

Stuart is once again leaning against the truck when Mitch is finally able to leave the grave site. The two men get in and make their way back into Twisted Timbers. Stuart is once again making small talk and yet again Mitch is paying little attention. There is something about driving through the Oregon hills that makes a passenger lose track of their surroundings and get lost in the view. Mitch remembers telling his father that these rolling hills looked like the pictures he would see of Ireland.

"Do you want me to take you home or back to the station?" Stuart has to ask the question several times before he is able to get a response from his passenger.

"I got a better idea. What do you say we stop down at The Bottom Dollar? I could go for a drink." Mitch has never been much of a drinking man, but drastic times call for drastic measures. He is more looking for a little company at the moment.

The request comes as a shock to Stuart. He quickly slows the car down and makes the turn onto Main Street. The sun is setting on a lazy Tuesday night in town. The sudden increase in visitors was a welcome surprise to the business owners of the town. The tourist season is still a few weeks away and the attention the news has given the town will surely cause a spike in business.

With a small grin Stuart looks over at Mitch as he parks outside the same bar where they had to arrest a former deputy. "Anything you say, Sheriff."

THE END

Kevin M. Moehring

Make sure to follow the author on Facebook at

https://facebook.com/kevinmmoehring

The best way you can help an Indie author is to leave a review and let other readers know what you thought about the book. Please return to the site where you purchased the book, and leave an honest review. Thanks for taking the time to read my latest story and be on the lookout for more releases in the Twisted Timbers series.

Kevin M. Moehring